REBEL JAIL: VOLUME 5

It is a time of drastic action for the Rebellion. Luke Skywalker, Han Solo, and Princess Leia have captured Darth Vader's secret ally, droid expert Dr. Aphra, in an effort to obtain Imperial information.

While the princess is securing Dr. Aphra at Sunspot Prison, a mysterious invader has seized control of the facility and begins eliminating prisoners. Cornered, Leia and Sana join forces with the doctor to release the inmates and spare them from an untimely death.

Meanwhile, Han and Luke have responded to Sana's distress call, arriving in time for the unknown attacker to reveal himself....

JASON AARON
Writer

LEINIL FRANCIS YU
Penciler

GERRY ALANGUILAN
Inker

SUNNY GHO & JAVA TARTAGLIA
Colorists

CHRIS ELIOPOULOS
Letterer

LEINIL YU & SUNNY GHO
Cover Artists

HEATHER ANTOS
Assistant Editor

JORDAN D. WHITE
Editor

C.B. CEBULSKI
Executive Editor

AXEL ALONSO
Editor In Chief

JOE QUESADA
Chief Creative Officer

DAN BUCKLEY
Publisher

For Lucasfilm:
Creative Director MICHAEL SIGLAIN
Senior Editor FRANK PARISI
Lucasfilm Story Group RAYNE ROBERTS, PABLO HIDALGO, LELAND CHEE, MATT MARTIN

ABDO
Spotlight

ABDOPUBLISHING.COM

Reinforced library bound edition published in 2018 by Spotlight,
a division of ABDO, PO Box 398166, Minneapolis, Minnesota 55439.
Spotlight produces high-quality reinforced library bound editions for
schools and libraries. Published by agreement with Marvel Characters, Inc.

Printed in the United States of America, North Mankato, Minnesota.
092017
012018

THIS BOOK CONTAINS
RECYCLED MATERIALS

marvelkids.com

STAR WARS © & TM 2018 LUCASFILM LTD.

PUBLISHER'S CATALOGING-IN-PUBLICATION DATA

Names: Aaron, Jason, author. | Mayhew, Mike; Yu, Leinil Francis; Alanguilan, Gerry;
    Gho, Sunny; Tartaglia, Java, illustrators.
Title: Rebel jail / writer: Jason Aaron ; art: Mike Mayhew; Leinil Francis Yu; Gerry
    Alanguilan; Sunny Gho; Java Tartaglia.
Description: Reinforced library bound edition. | Minneapolis, MN : Spotlight, 2018 |
    Series: Star Wars: Rebel jail | Volume 1 written by Jason Aaron ; illustrated by
    Mike Mayhew. | Volumes 2 and 4 written by Jason Aaron ; illustrated by Leinil
    Francis Yu; Gerry Alanguilan & Sunny Gho. | Volume 3 written by Jason Aaron ;
    illustrated by Leinil Francis Yu & Sunny Gho. | Volume 5 written by Jason Aaron ;
    illustrated by Leinil Francis Yu; Gerry Alanguilan; Sunny Gho & Java Tartaglia.
Summary: During Ben Kenobi's exile on Tatooine, he vows to keep a young Luke
    safe; Princess Leia and Sana Starros bring an important captive to the Sunspot
    Prison, where they are ambushed by a rebel spy on a mission of life and death;
    Luke Skywalker tries his hand at smuggling after Han loses their rebel funds in a
    gamble.
Identifiers: LCCN 2017941922 | ISBN 9781532141416 (volume 1) | ISBN
    9781532141423 (volume 2) | ISBN 9781532141430 (volume 3) | ISBN
    9781532141447 (volume 4) | ISBN 9781532141454 (volume 5)
Subjects: LCSH: Star Wars (film)--Juvenile fiction. | Adventure and Adventurers--
    Juvenile fiction. | Graphic Novels--Juvenile fiction.
Classification: DDC 741.5--dc23
LC record available at http://lccn.loc.gov/2017941922

Spotlight

A Division of ABDO
abdopublishing.com

STAR WARS

REBEL JAIL

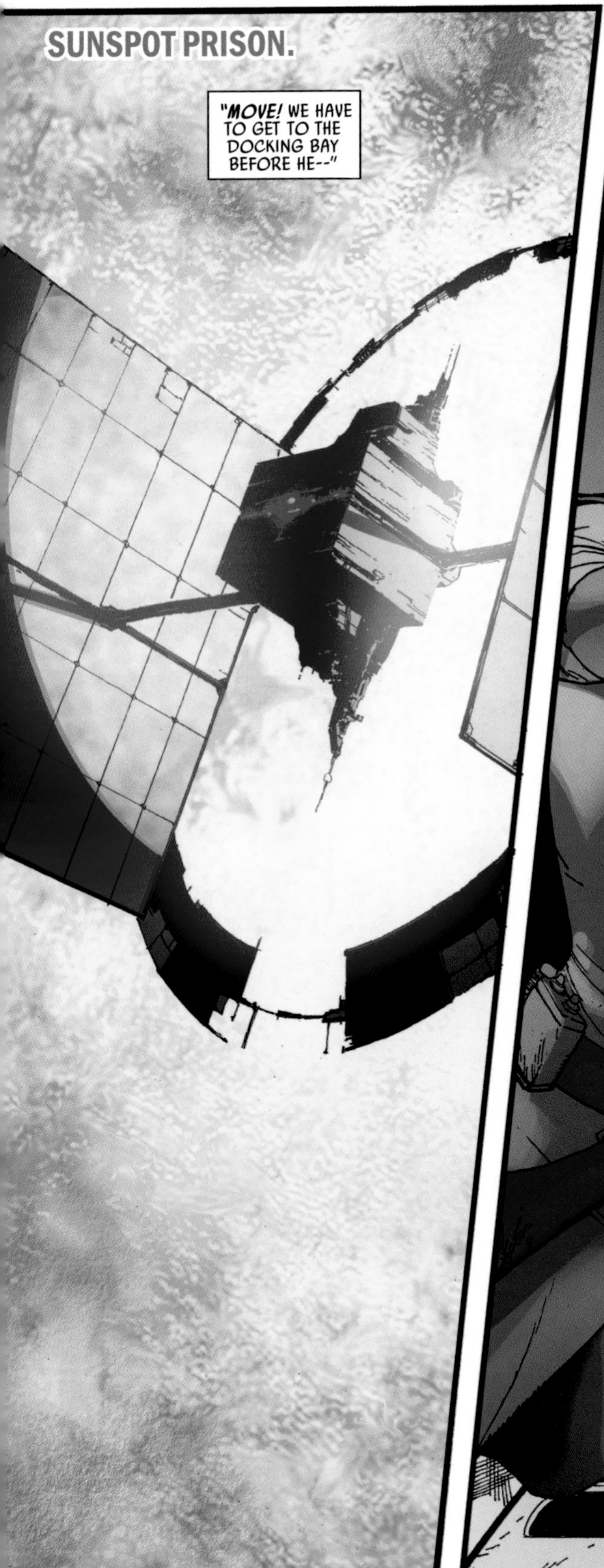
SUNSPOT PRISON.
"MOVE! WE HAVE TO GET TO THE DOCKING BAY BEFORE HE--"

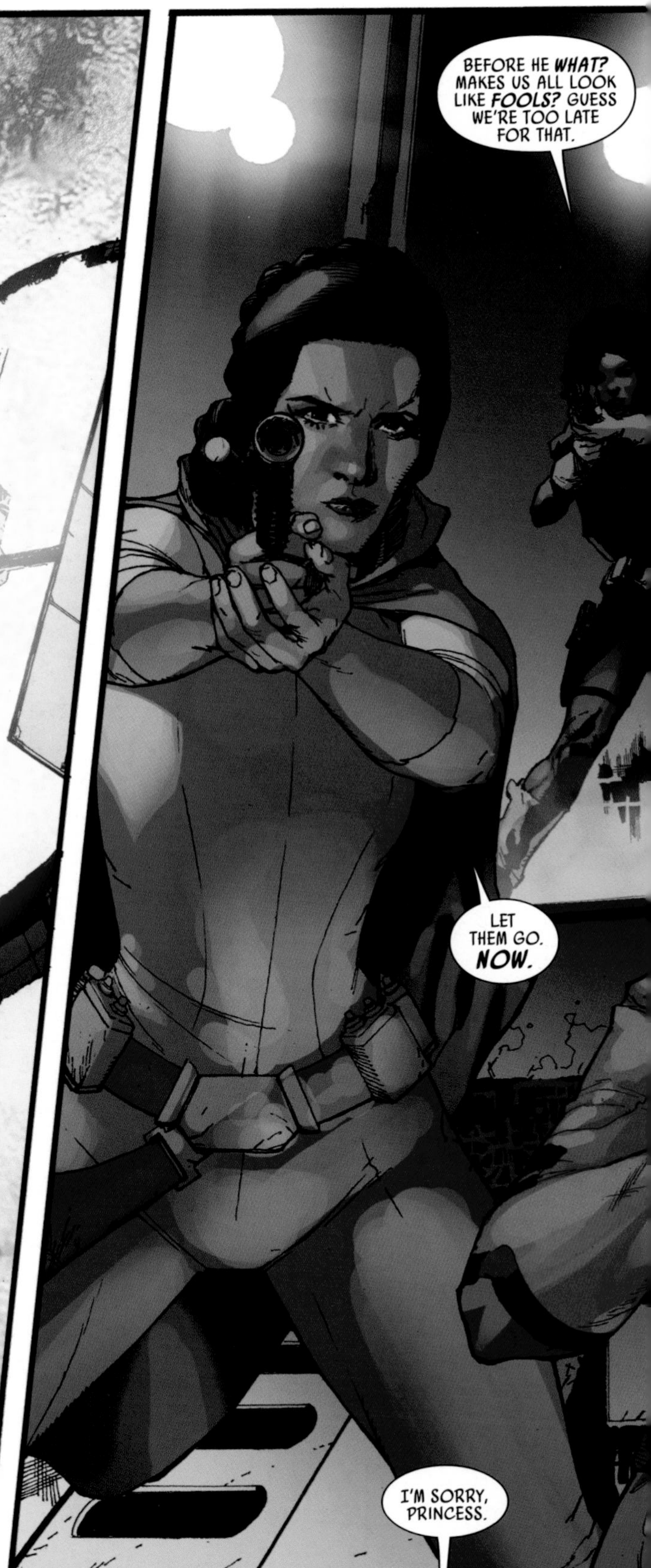
BEFORE HE WHAT? MAKES US ALL LOOK LIKE FOOLS? GUESS WE'RE TOO LATE FOR THAT.
LET THEM GO. NOW.
I'M SORRY, PRINCESS.

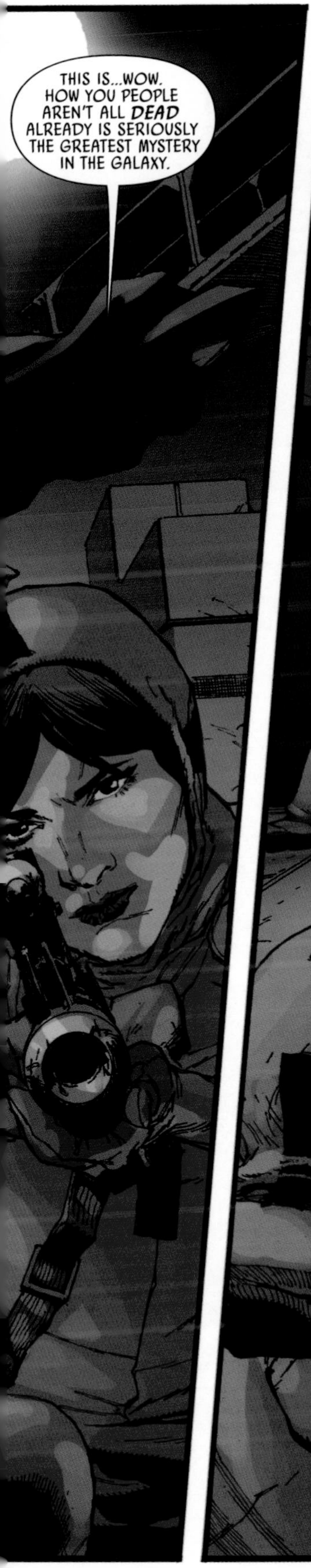
THIS IS...WOW. HOW YOU PEOPLE AREN'T ALL DEAD ALREADY IS SERIOUSLY THE GREATEST MYSTERY IN THE GALAXY.

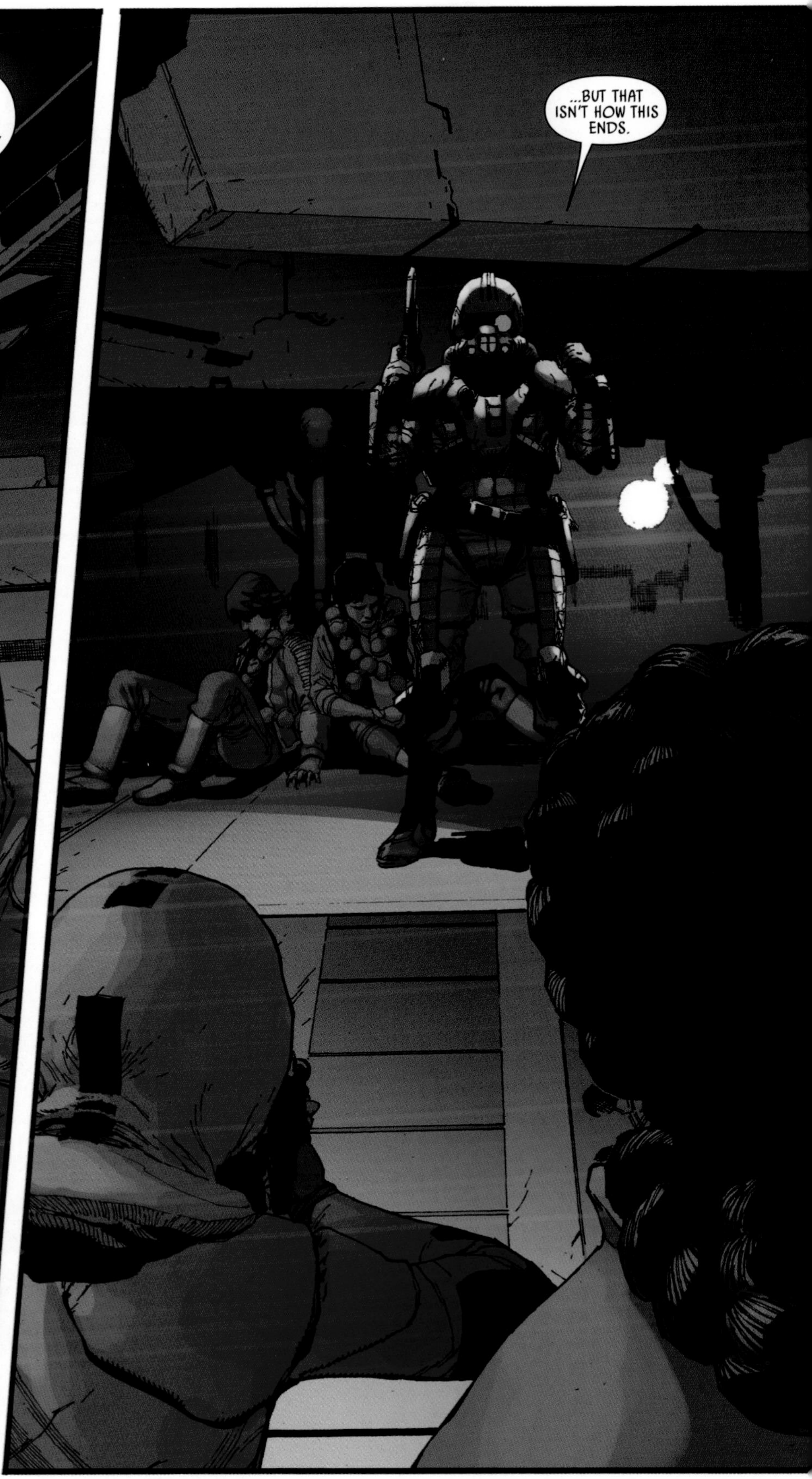
...BUT THAT ISN'T HOW THIS ENDS.

THIS IS YOUR LAST CHANCE TO ACCEPT WHAT I'VE BEEN TRYING TO SHOW YOU, PRINCESS LEIA.

I WANT YOU TO *WIN* THIS WAR, I REALLY DO. I WANT TO SEE THE EMPIRE FALL. I WANT TO GIVE YOU THE TOOLS YOU NEED FOR VICTORY.

WHETHER YOUR FRIENDS HERE BECOME *CASUALTIES* IN THAT WAR IS ENTIRELY UP TO YOU.

DON'T DO IT.

DON'T HURT THEM. LOOK, I'LL PUT MY BLASTER DOWN, AND THEN WE CAN TALK ABOUT...

I DON'T WANT YOU TO PUT IT DOWN. I WANT YOU TO *USE* IT.

I WANT YOU TO SHOW ME YOU HAVE WHAT IT TAKES TO LEAD THE REBELLION.

YOU HAVE AN *IMPERIAL PRISONER* IN YOUR MIDST.

SHOOT HER, AND I'LL LET YOUR FRIENDS GO FREE.

WAIT, *WHAT?*

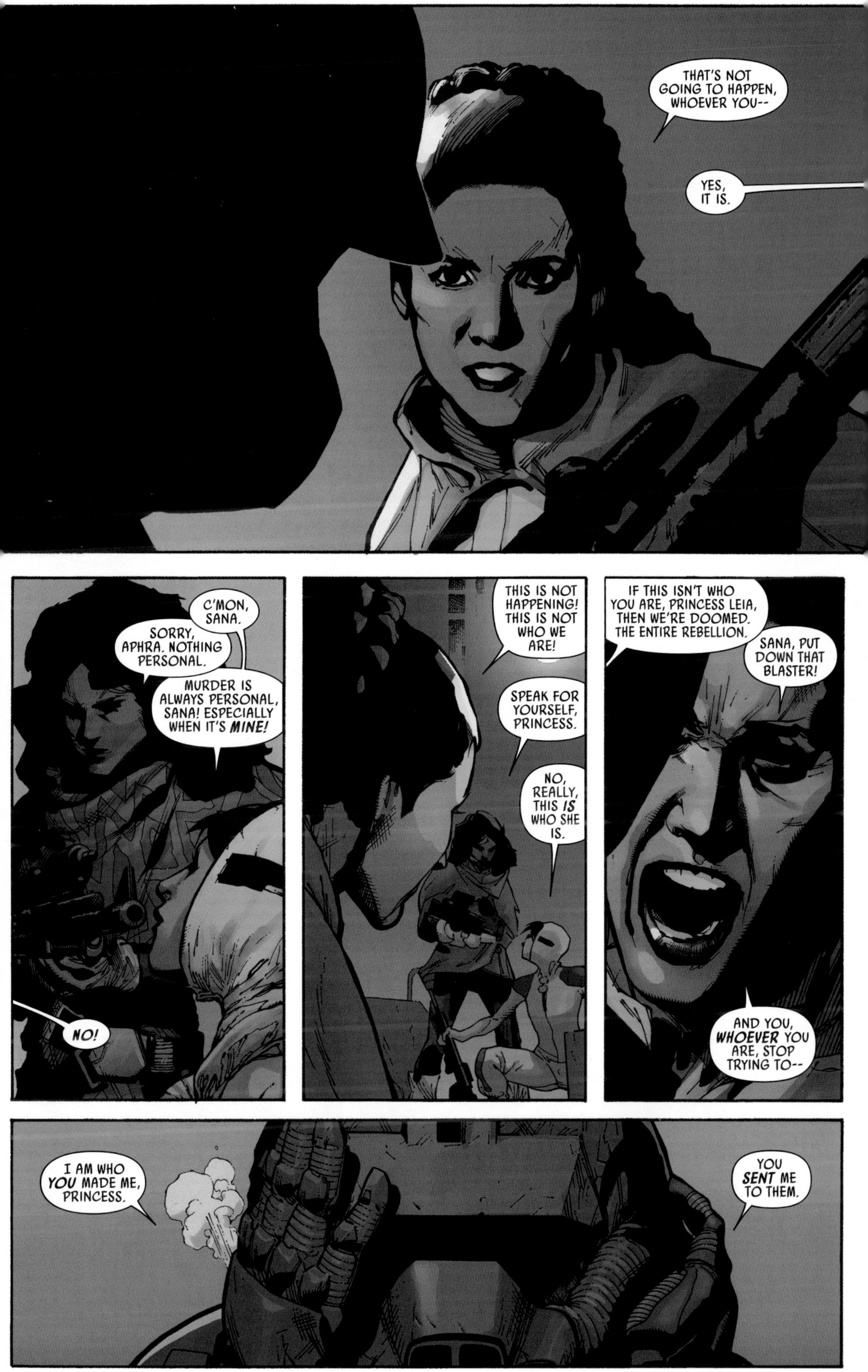
THAT'S NOT GOING TO HAPPEN, WHOEVER YOU--
YES, IT IS.
C'MON, SANA.
SORRY, APHRA. NOTHING PERSONAL.
MURDER IS ALWAYS PERSONAL, SANA! ESPECIALLY WHEN IT'S MINE!
NO!
THIS IS NOT HAPPENING! THIS IS NOT WHO WE ARE!
SPEAK FOR YOURSELF, PRINCESS.
NO, REALLY, THIS IS WHO SHE IS.
IF THIS ISN'T WHO YOU ARE, PRINCESS LEIA, THEN WE'RE DOOMED. THE ENTIRE REBELLION.
SANA, PUT DOWN THAT BLASTER!
AND YOU, WHOEVER YOU ARE, STOP TRYING TO--
I AM WHO YOU MADE ME, PRINCESS.
YOU SENT ME TO THEM.

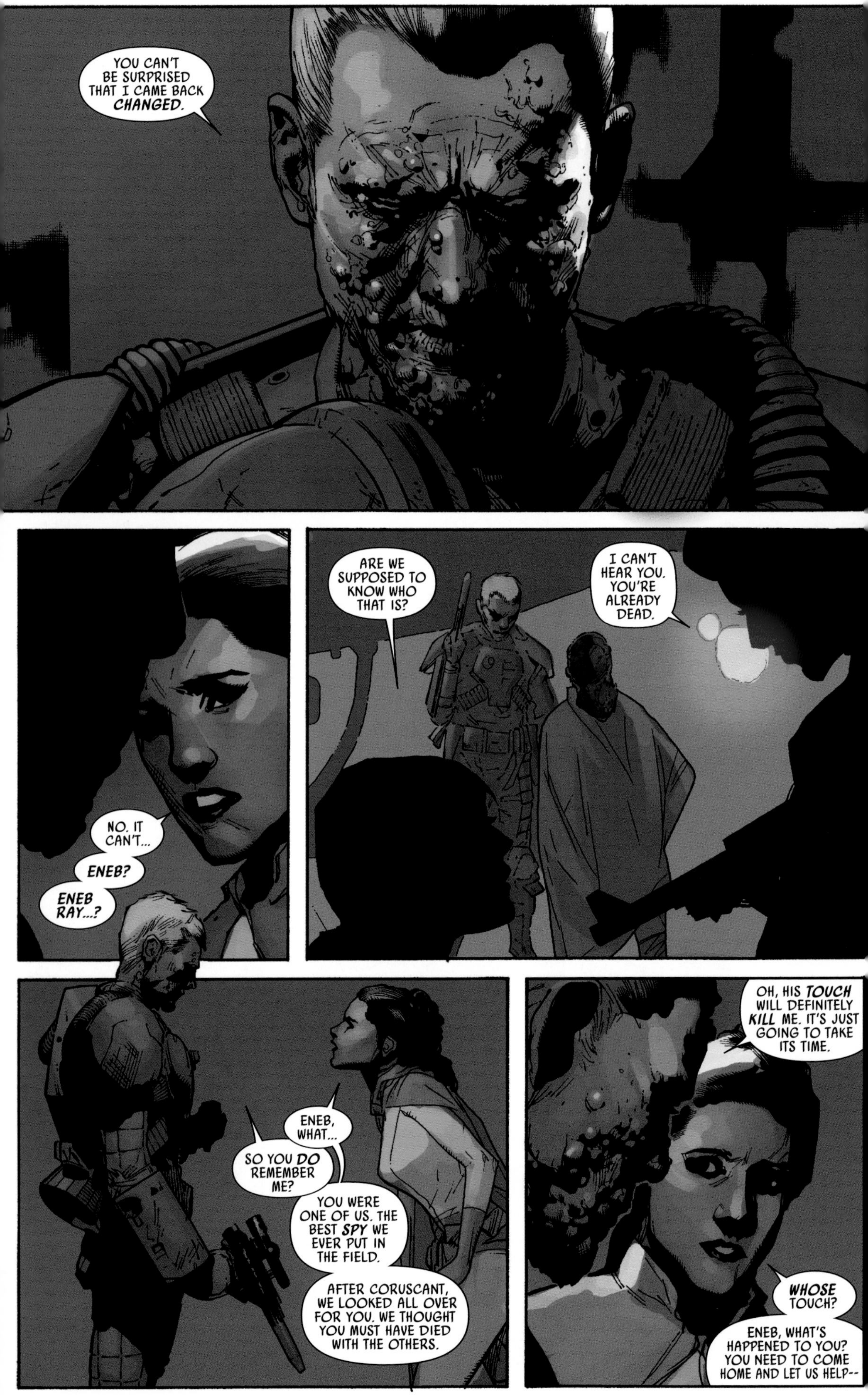
YOU CAN'T BE SURPRISED THAT I CAME BACK *CHANGED.*
NO. IT CAN'T...
ENEB?
ENEB RAY...?
ARE WE SUPPOSED TO KNOW WHO THAT IS?
I CAN'T HEAR YOU. YOU'RE ALREADY DEAD.
ENEB, WHAT...
SO YOU *DO* REMEMBER ME?
YOU WERE ONE OF US. THE BEST *SPY* WE EVER PUT IN THE FIELD.
AFTER CORUSCANT, WE LOOKED ALL OVER FOR YOU. WE THOUGHT YOU MUST HAVE DIED WITH THE OTHERS.
OH, HIS *TOUCH* WILL DEFINITELY *KILL* ME. IT'S JUST GOING TO TAKE ITS TIME.
WHOSE TOUCH?
ENEB, WHAT'S HAPPENED TO YOU? YOU NEED TO COME HOME AND LET US HELP--

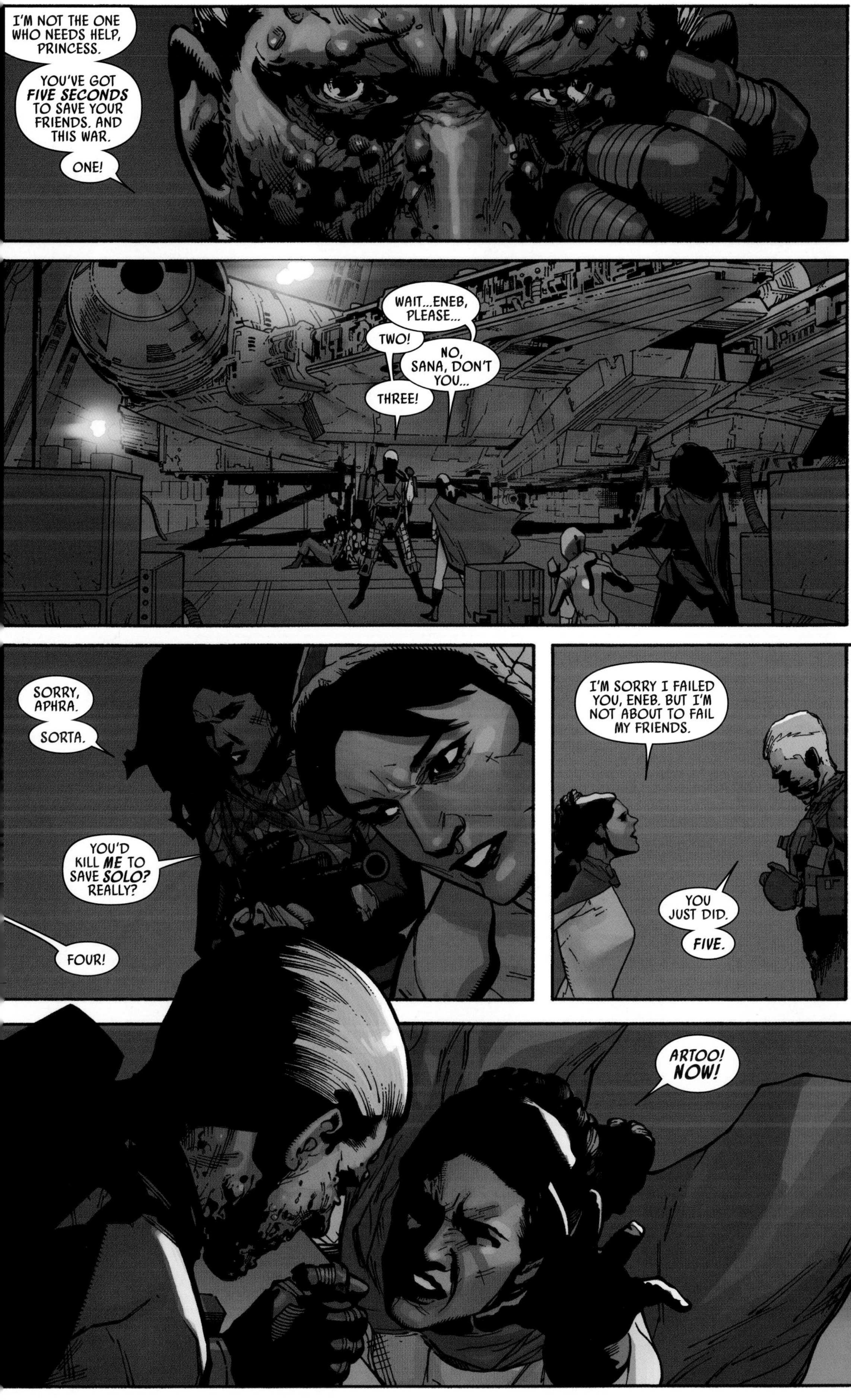
I'M NOT THE ONE WHO NEEDS HELP, PRINCESS.
YOU'VE GOT FIVE SECONDS TO SAVE YOUR FRIENDS. AND THIS WAR.
ONE!
WAIT...ENEB, PLEASE...
TWO!
NO, SANA, DON'T YOU...
THREE!
SORRY, APHRA.
SORTA.
YOU'D KILL ME TO SAVE SOLO? REALLY?
FOUR!
I'M SORRY I FAILED YOU, ENEB. BUT I'M NOT ABOUT TO FAIL MY FRIENDS.
YOU JUST DID.
FIVE.
ARTOO! NOW!

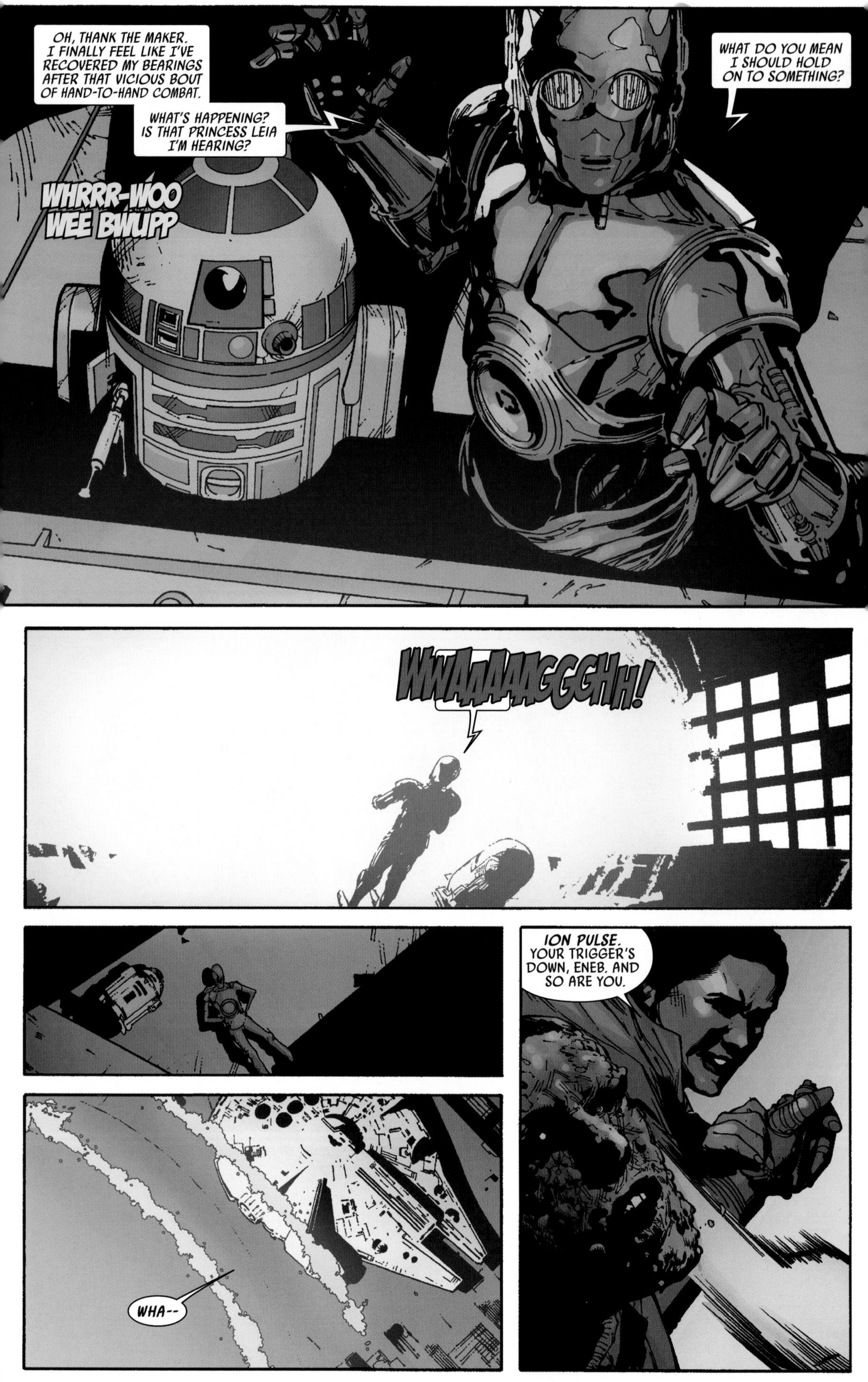

OH, THANK THE MAKER. I FINALLY FEEL LIKE I'VE RECOVERED MY BEARINGS AFTER THAT VICIOUS BOUT OF HAND-TO-HAND COMBAT.
WHAT'S HAPPENING? IS THAT PRINCESS LEIA I'M HEARING?
WHRRR-WOO WEE BWUPP
WHAT DO YOU MEAN I SHOULD HOLD ON TO SOMETHING?
WWAAAAAAGGGHH!
WHA--
ION PULSE. YOUR TRIGGER'S DOWN, ENEB. AND SO ARE YOU.

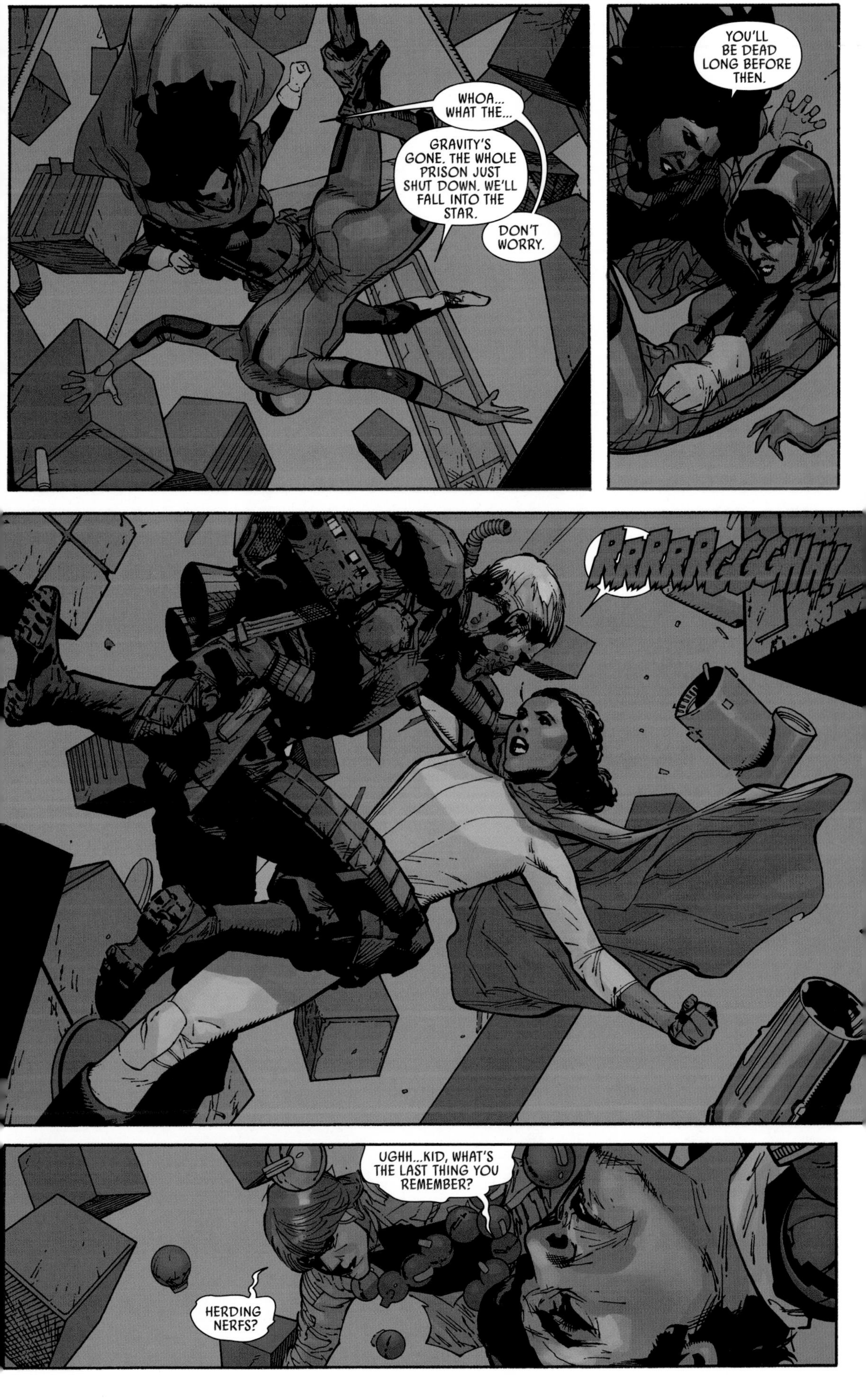
WHOA... WHAT THE...
GRAVITY'S GONE. THE WHOLE PRISON JUST SHUT DOWN. WE'LL FALL INTO THE STAR.
DON'T WORRY.
YOU'LL BE DEAD LONG BEFORE THEN.
RRRRRGGGHH!
UGHH...KID, WHAT'S THE LAST THING YOU REMEMBER?
HERDING NERFS?

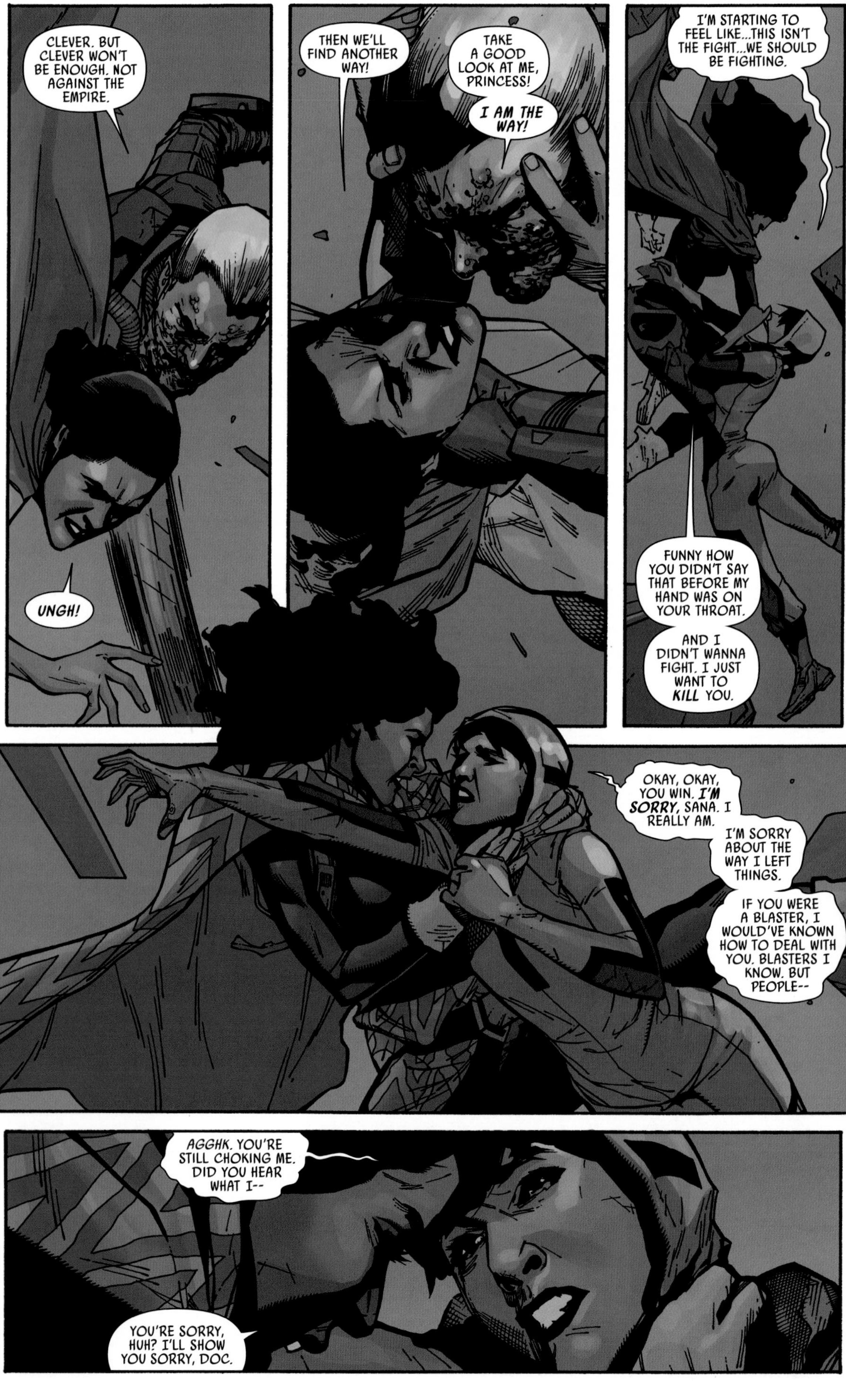
CLEVER. BUT CLEVER WON'T BE ENOUGH. NOT AGAINST THE EMPIRE.
UNGH!
THEN WE'LL FIND ANOTHER WAY!
TAKE A GOOD LOOK AT ME, PRINCESS!
I AM THE WAY!
I'M STARTING TO FEEL LIKE...THIS ISN'T THE FIGHT...WE SHOULD BE FIGHTING.
FUNNY HOW YOU DIDN'T SAY THAT BEFORE MY HAND WAS ON YOUR THROAT.
AND I DIDN'T WANNA FIGHT. I JUST WANT TO KILL YOU.
OKAY, OKAY, YOU WIN. I'M SORRY, SANA. I REALLY AM.
I'M SORRY ABOUT THE WAY I LEFT THINGS.
IF YOU WERE A BLASTER, I WOULD'VE KNOWN HOW TO DEAL WITH YOU. BLASTERS I KNOW. BUT PEOPLE--
AGGHK. YOU'RE STILL CHOKING ME. DID YOU HEAR WHAT I--
YOU'RE SORRY, HUH? I'LL SHOW YOU SORRY, DOC.

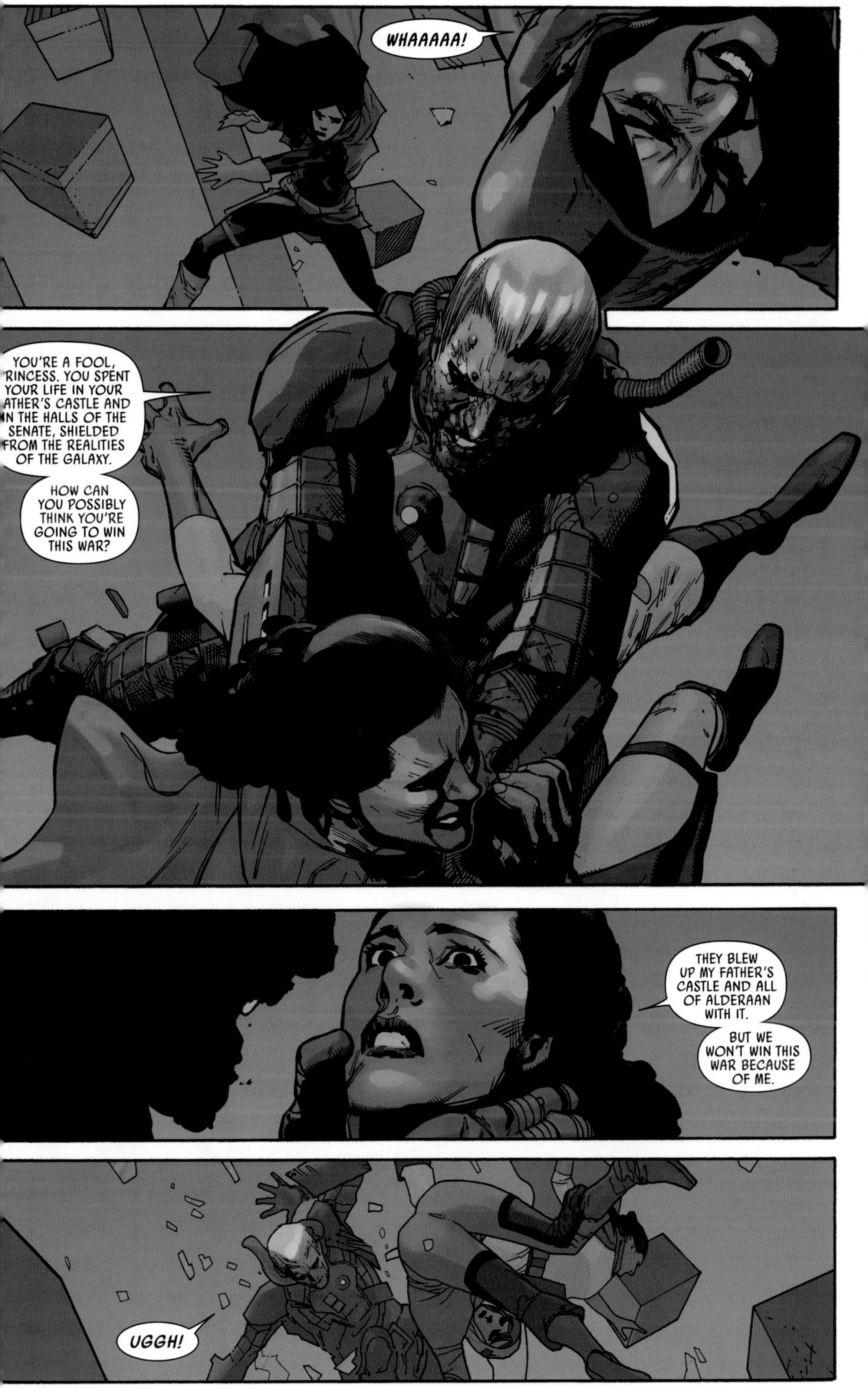

WHAAAAA!
YOU'RE A FOOL, RINCESS. YOU SPENT YOUR LIFE IN YOUR ATHER'S CASTLE AND IN THE HALLS OF THE SENATE, SHIELDED FROM THE REALITIES OF THE GALAXY.
HOW CAN YOU POSSIBLY THINK YOU'RE GOING TO WIN THIS WAR?
THEY BLEW UP MY FATHER'S CASTLE AND ALL OF ALDERAAN WITH IT.
BUT WE WON'T WIN THIS WAR BECAUSE OF ME.
UGGH!

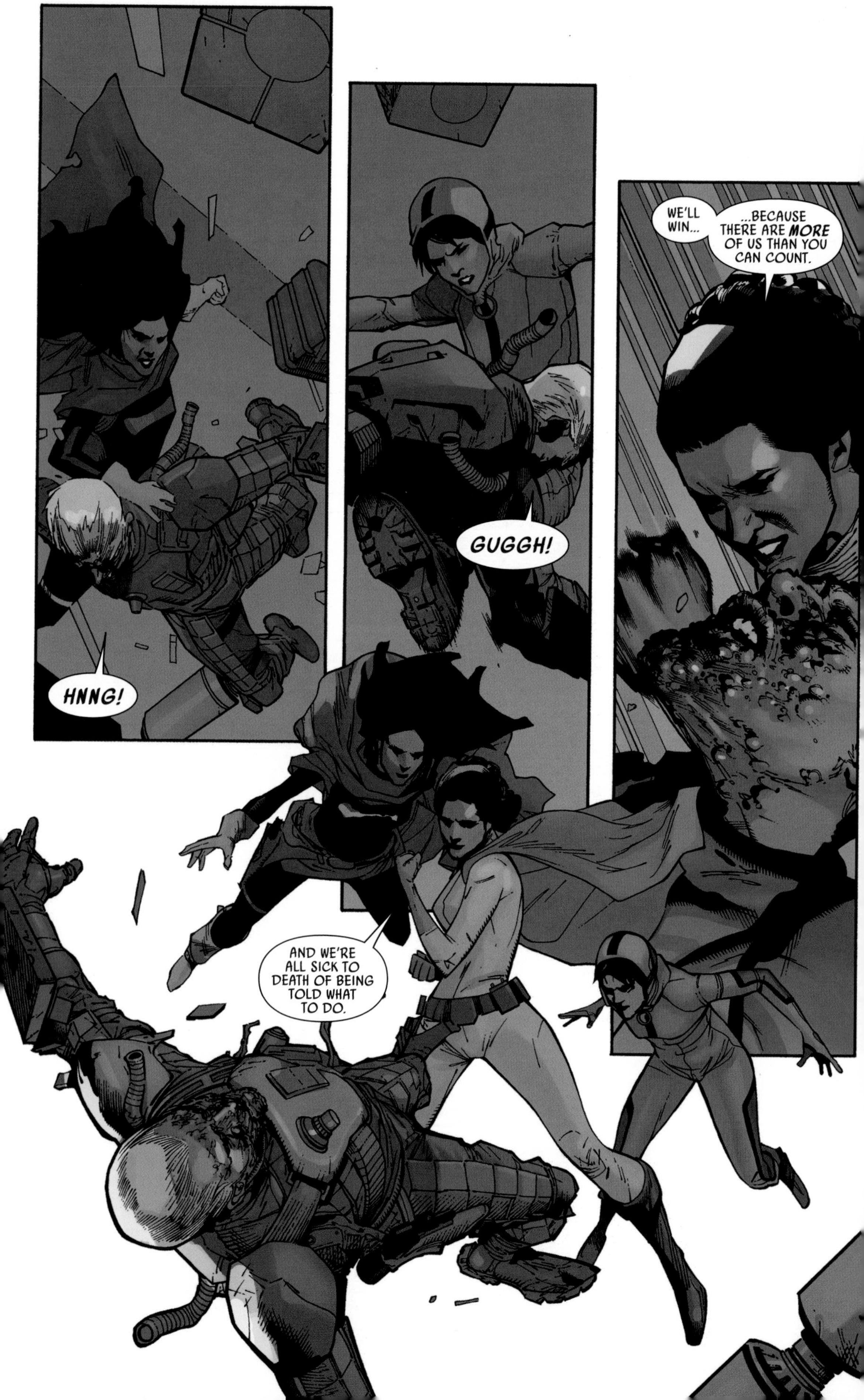
HNNG!
GUGGH!
WE'LL WIN...
...BECAUSE THERE ARE MORE OF US THAN YOU CAN COUNT.
AND WE'RE ALL SICK TO DEATH OF BEING TOLD WHAT TO DO.

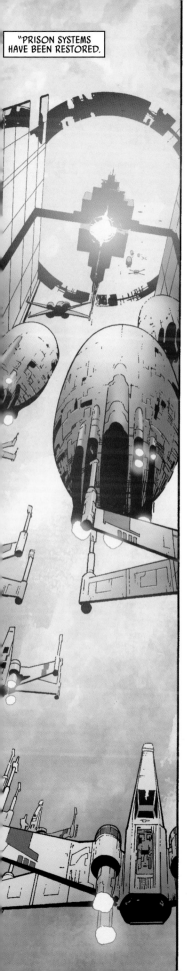

"PRISON SYSTEMS HAVE BEEN RESTORED.

"AND THE EVACUATION HAS BEGUN."

THANKS TO YOU, PRINCESS... THERE ARE STILL *SOME* OF US LEFT TO EVACUATE.

BUT NOT ENOUGH. TOO MANY PEOPLE DIED HERE TODAY, WARDEN. GUARDS AND PRISONERS BOTH.

YES, PRINCESS. WE'RE DOING OUR BEST TO ACCOUNT FOR ALL OF THE REMAINING INMATES. BUT, AH...

I'M AFRAID THERE IS *ONE* THAT SEEMS TO HAVE BEEN MISPLACED.

GET AWAY FROM THE ESCAPE POD, DR. APHRA.

OH, C'MON.

I SAVED YOUR LIFE LIKE *FIVE TIMES* TODAY! WAY MORE IF YOU COUNT ALL THE TIMES I DIDN'T KILL YOU WHEN I REALLY WANTED TO.

THAT DOESN'T CHANGE THE FACT THAT YOU'RE A *PRISONER* HERE. I CAN'T JUST LET YOU WALK AWAY.

UM, YES, YOU DEFINITELY COULD.

WHAT IF I PROMISE TO BE *GOOD?* OR...YOU KNOW... AT LEAST BETTER THAN USUAL?

THIS IS NO GAME, DOCTOR. I HOPE YOU REALIZE JUST HOW DANGEROUS *DARTH VADER* REALLY IS.

NO MATTER HOW USEFUL YOU ARE TO HIM NOW, SOONER OR LATER HE WILL GET AROUND TO KILLING YOU.

AND WHEN THAT DAY COMES, IF YOU SHOULD HAPPEN TO SOMEHOW SURVIVE...

...I SUGGEST YOU LOOK ME UP.

WAIT, BUT... WHAT ARE YOU SAYING?

I SAID I COULDN'T LET YOU WALK AWAY.

I DIDN'T SAY ANYTHING ABOUT *HER.*

WHU...

ESCAPE POD ACTIVATED.

AND DON'T EVER COME BACK.

HOW LONG BEFORE SHE FINDS ALL THE *TRACKERS* WE HID IN HER CLOTHES?

ABOUT AS LONG AS IT'LL TAKE US TO FIND THE ONES SHE HID ON OUR SHIP.

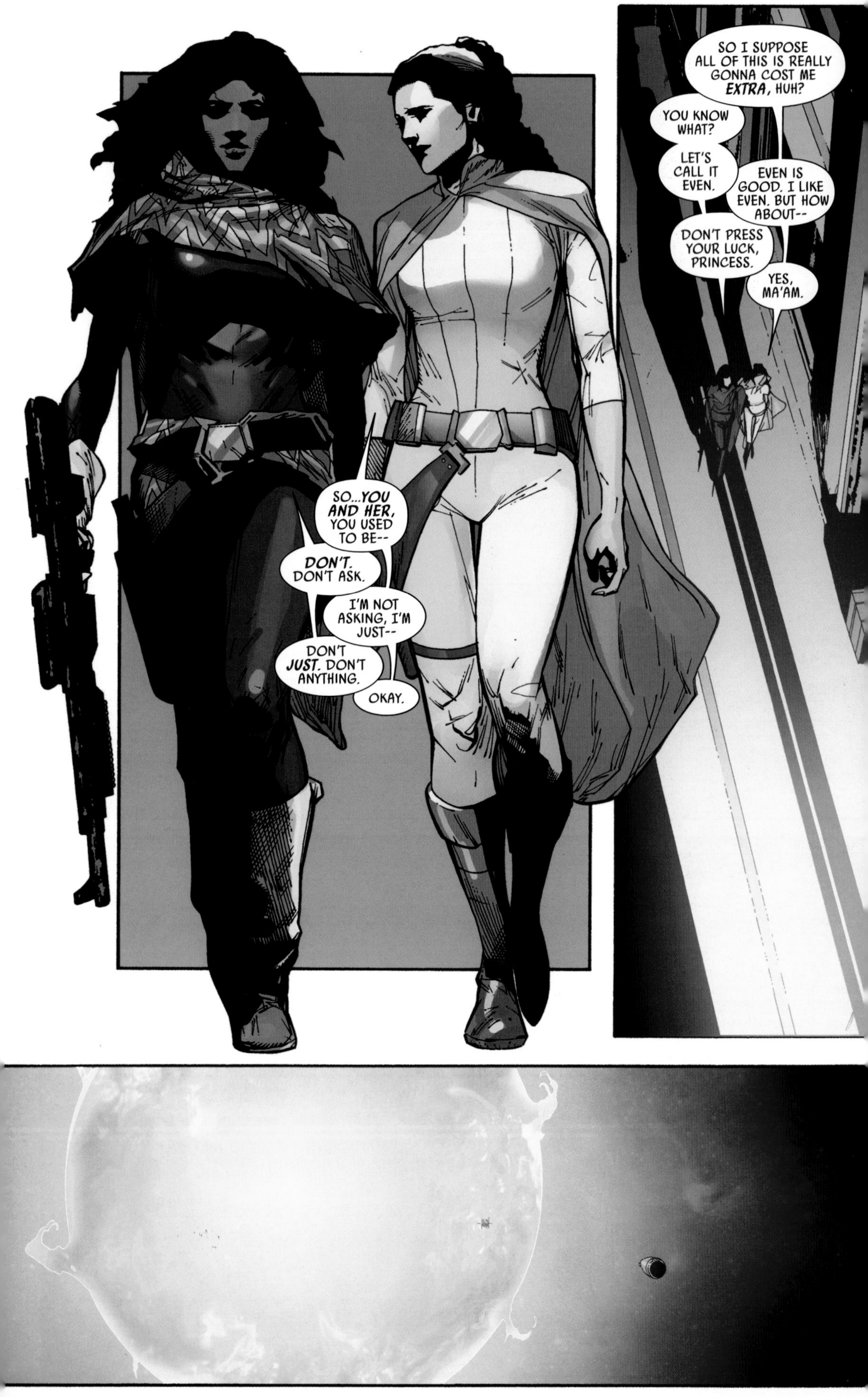
SO...YOU AND HER, YOU USED TO BE--
DON'T. DON'T ASK.
I'M NOT ASKING, I'M JUST--
DON'T JUST. DON'T ANYTHING.
OKAY.
SO I SUPPOSE ALL OF THIS IS REALLY GONNA COST ME EXTRA, HUH?
YOU KNOW WHAT?
LET'S CALL IT EVEN.
EVEN IS GOOD. I LIKE EVEN. BUT HOW ABOUT--
DON'T PRESS YOUR LUCK, PRINCESS.
YES, MA'AM.

YES, I **AM** GOING TO REQUEST A TRANSFER. I HEARD FROM AN ARFIVE UNIT ONBOARD THE REBEL FLEET THAT THEY'RE LOOKING FOR PROTOCOL DROIDS AT THE ALLIANCE RECORDS OFFICE ON FUSAI.

TRANSLATIONS AND DATAWORK ARE A LITTLE BIT MORE MY SPEED. NO ONE EVER HAD THEIR ARMS PULLED OFF WHILE RECORD KEEPING.

BWOOP BWIP WADDA WERP

NO, YOU **CAN'T** COME. THEY HAVE NO OPENINGS FOR MOP BUCKETS.

THAT WAS NOT OUR BEST RESCUE. WE JUST MIGHT BE WORSE AT RESCUES THAN WE ARE AT SMUGGLING, HAN.

REMEMBER, LUKE, NOT A WORD TO ANYONE ABOUT THE...YOU KNOW.

THE WHAT?

EXACTLY.

YOU TWO ARE TERRIBLE AT RESCUES.

NICE TO SEE YOU TOO, SANA. HEY, IT LOOKS LIKE YOU AND LEIA ARE REALLY STARTING TO--

I GOT TO FLY THE **FALCON!**

HAN, TELL THIS KID HE'S NOT OLD ENOUGH TO TALK TO ME.

MOTHER OF MOONS... IT SMELLS LIKE A **HERD OF NERFS** IN HERE!

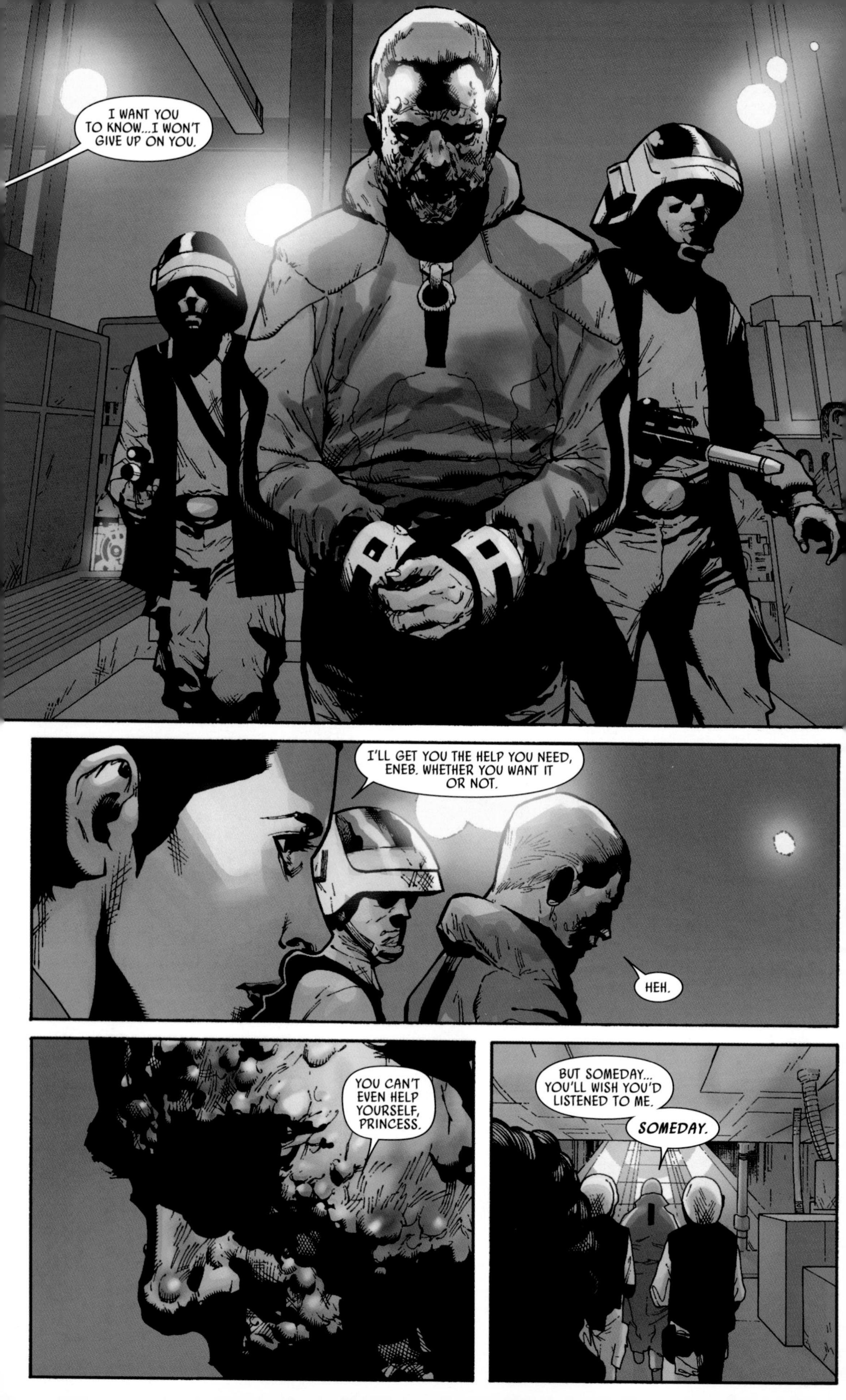
I WANT YOU TO KNOW...I WON'T GIVE UP ON YOU.
I'LL GET YOU THE HELP YOU NEED, ENEB. WHETHER YOU WANT IT OR NOT.
HEH.
YOU CAN'T EVEN HELP YOURSELF, PRINCESS.
BUT SOMEDAY... YOU'LL WISH YOU'D LISTENED TO ME.
SOMEDAY.

"SOMEDAY YOU'LL REALIZE WHAT IT IS YOU'RE REALLY FIGHTING.

"AND HOW YOU HAVE NO HOPE OF ACTUALLY WINNING.

"YOU'LL REALIZE... ONLY BECAUSE THEY'VE COME FOR YOU.

"WITH A FORCE AND A FURY YOU CAN'T BEGIN TO IMAGINE.

"REMEMBER ME ON THAT DAY, PRINCESS.

"REMEMBER ME IN YOUR SCREAMS."

THIS WAS IT, ALL RIGHT. THIS WAS THE PRISON WHERE THEY WERE KEEPING KOLAR LUDD. I'D BET MY FAVORITE BLASTER ON IT.

BUT THEY'VE STRIPPED THE PLACE CLEAN. LEFT IT TO FALL INTO THE STAR.

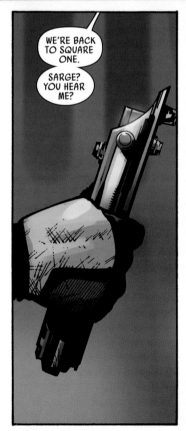

WE'RE BACK TO SQUARE ONE.

SARGE? YOU HEAR ME?

DOESN'T MATTER.

ORDERS JUST CAME IN.

WE'VE GOT A NEW MISSION.

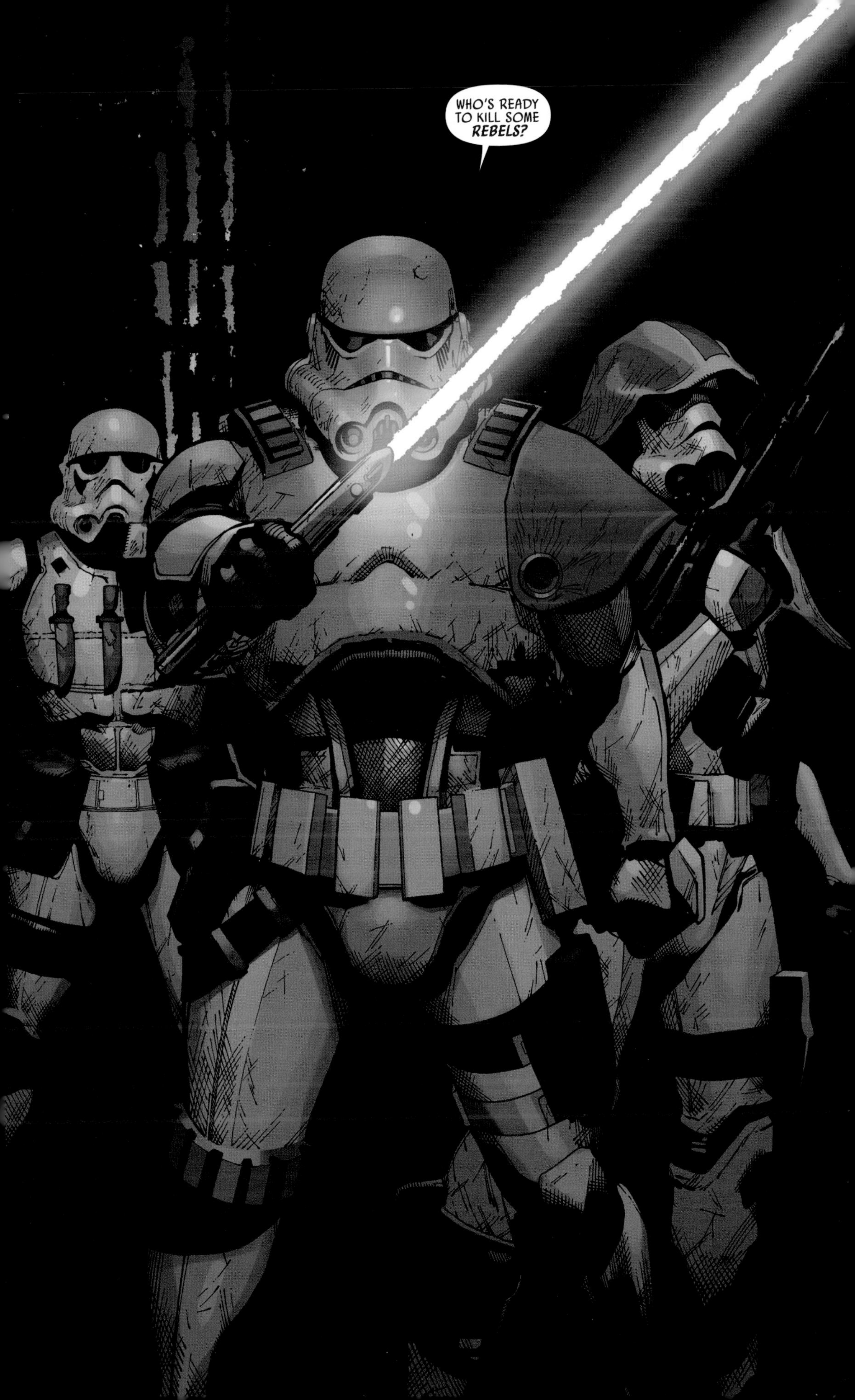
WHO'S READY TO KILL SOME REBELS?

REBEL JAIL

COLLECT THEM ALL!

Set of 5 Hardcover Books ISBN: 978-1-5321-4140-9

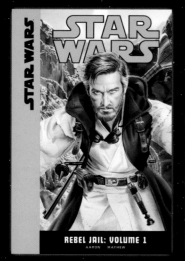

Hardcover Book ISBN
978-1-5321-4141-6

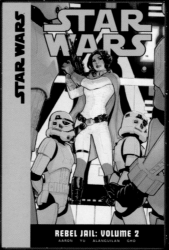

Hardcover Book ISBN
978-1-5321-4142-3

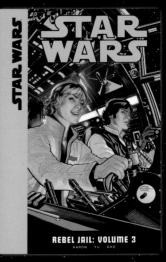

Hardcover Book ISBN
978-1-5321-4143-0

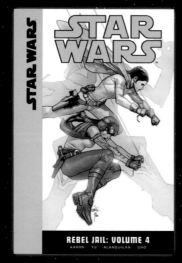

Hardcover Book ISBN
978-1-5321-4144-7

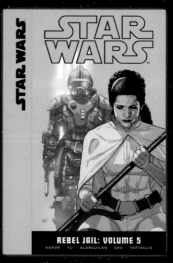

Hardcover Book ISBN
978-1-5321-4145-4

What Readers Are Saying About Lean from the Trenches

FANTASTIC! I know it's going to make a big dent in the world of software development. It's easily the most important book I have seen in the past year!

➤ **Mary Poppendieck, Author of the *Lean Software Development* series**

I read the whole thing end to end. In a word, FANTASTIC! Grounded, real, funny, easy to read, smooth flow, good balance between theory and practice.

➤ **Kent Beck**

Awesome. Kudos to you for documenting the everyday sort of decision making that has to happen for a big project to be successful. I hope it becomes a benchmark against which many more projects are judged.

➤ **Ward Cunningham**

I could not stop reading *Lean from the Trenches*. This book shows me that a big project can be run in a lean and agile way. For people in the trenches of large enterprises, stories like this make a huge difference.

➤ **Yves Hanoulle, Change Artist at PairCoaching.net**

An excellent peek into a pragmatic application of the best of the agile processes in a real-world scenario. If you ever wondered "Am I doing it right?" then this book may just provide you with the answer. Every technical team lead interested in seeing how an agile process actually works should buy this now!

➤ **Colin Yates, Principle Engineer, QFI Consulting LLP, UK**

It rocks. Finally, a nonpuritan, pragmatic, successful case study with real, usable ideas.

➤ **Simon Cromarty, The Agile Pirate**

I really enjoyed this immensely pragmatic and readable look at a real project organized on agile and lean principles. The emphasis on real-life experiences rather than theory was refreshing and engaging. I will definitely recommend this book to friends and will use its insights in my own professional engagements.

➤ **Kevin Beam, Independent Software Developer, Lambda42, LLC**

Lean from the Trenches

Managing Large-Scale Projects with Kanban

Henrik Kniberg

The Pragmatic Bookshelf

Dallas, Texas • Raleigh, North Carolina

Many of the designations used by manufacturers and sellers to distinguish their products are claimed as trademarks. Where those designations appear in this book, and The Pragmatic Programmers, LLC was aware of a trademark claim, the designations have been printed in initial capital letters or in all capitals. The Pragmatic Starter Kit, The Pragmatic Programmer, Pragmatic Programming, Pragmatic Bookshelf, PragProg and the linking *g* device are trademarks of The Pragmatic Programmers, LLC.

Every precaution was taken in the preparation of this book. However, the publisher assumes no responsibility for errors or omissions, or for damages that may result from the use of information (including program listings) contained herein.

Our Pragmatic courses, workshops, and other products can help you and your team create better software and have more fun. For more information, as well as the latest Pragmatic titles, please visit us at *http://pragprog.com*.

The team that produced this book includes:

Kay Keppler (editor)
Potomac Indexing, LLC (indexer)
Kim Wimpsett (copyeditor)
David J Kelly (typesetter)
Janet Furlow (producer)
Juliet Benda (rights)
Ellie Callahan (support)

Printed in the United States of America.
ISBN-13: 978-1-934356-85-2
Printed on acid-free paper.
Book version: P1.0—December, 2011

Contents

Foreword

We who give project advice are faced with a mighty temptation. The teams who engage us are looking for direction, hope, ideas, energy, and guidance (and sometimes someone to blame, but that's a different topic). We are called in because we have been in a variety of situations, some more functional and some less. We try to help our clients move toward "more functional." However, we are often as baffled as they about what to do next.

The temptation I am referring to is the temptation to begin speaking beyond our experience, to meet the client's need for certainty by manufacturing a certainty we ourselves do not feel. Left untreated, this results in dogma, revealed by words like "must," "always," and "everybody."

One beauty of this book's story is its complete lack of dogma. It is a story. A story of a project that had real troubles and addressed them with a small set of easily understood practices. Applying those practices required wisdom, patience, and persistence, which is why you can't just copy the story to fix your project.

The other reason you can't just copy the story is because it isn't written as a general prescription. It is a particular team in a particular culture with a particular client. You are going to have to work to apply it to your situation, but that's good, because you are in any case going to have to work to encourage any change.

There are general principles at work here. I've been fortunate enough to work with Henrik a bit, and he told me he really has only one trick: make all the important information visible in one place and then decide what to do together. If that's his only trick (and I have my doubts), it's a good one.

Society has learned to distrust us for our big, complicated, and ultimately futile public software projects. This is the story of a public service project that managed to serve the public. What it takes to regain the public's trust is teamwork, transparency, and early and frequent releases. Oops, I just succumbed to that temptation I just warned you about. You'd better just read the story and learn your own lessons.

Kent Beck
September 2011

Preface

Many of us have heard about Lean software development, Kanban, and other trendy buzzwords. But what does this stuff actually look like in practice? And how does it scale to a 60-person project developing a really complex system?

I can't tell you how to do it, since every context is different. But I will tell you how we've been doing it (basically a Scrum-XP-Kanban hybrid), and maybe some of our solutions and lessons learned can be valuable in your context.

Who This Book Is For

This book is primarily written for team leads, managers, coaches, and other change agents within software development organizations.

However, some parts will probably be useful to anyone interested in software development, Lean product development, or collaboration techniques in general—regardless of role or industry.

For those who want to comment, go to the book's main page,[1] and from there you can reach the forum and errata pages. I welcome your comments!

How to Read This Book

This book is divided in two parts, each subdivided into several short chapters.

Part I, "How We Work," is a case study showing how Kanban and Lean principles were applied in a large project for the Swedish police. The first chapter describes what the project was about, and the subsequent chapters describe specific challenges (such as scaling), how we dealt with those challenges, and what we learned along the way.

Part II, "A Closer Look at the Techniques," starts with a high-level introduction to Agile and Lean and then expands on some of the practices mentioned in Part I, such as cause-effect diagrams.

---

1. http://pragprog.com/book/hklean/lean-from-the-trenches

I suggest you read Part I end to end, since that is the heart of this book, and the chapters build upon each other. Then you can cherry-pick from Part II, since those chapters are independent.

New to Agile or Lean?

If you are new to Agile or Lean, don't worry. This book is all about practice, not theory. I'll simply show you what we've been doing, and you'll pick up most of the theory along the way.

If you prefer to start with a high-level overview of Agile and Lean and the associated methods Scrum, XP, and Kanban, then go ahead and jump to Chapter 17, *Agile and Lean in a Nutshell*, on page 103.

Disclaimer

I don't claim that our way of working is perfectly Lean. Lean is a direction, not a place. It's all about continuous improvement. *Lean* has no clear definition, but many of the practices that we apply are based on the principles of Lean product development that Mary Poppendieck, David Anderson, and Don Reinertsen teach. And these practices, by the way, happen to match Agile principles quite well on most counts.

Another thing—you will see this project from my perspective, a part-time coach during six months of this project. My goal is not to present a 100 percent complete picture; I'll just give you a general idea of what we've been doing and what we've learned so far.

Acknowledgments

Many people have contributed to this book—thanks to you all! I'd especially like to thank Håkan Rydman for being the internal change agent and getting me into this project, and Tomas Alsterlund for providing strong management support and keeping us focused on the project goal.

And I'd also like to call out the following people:

Christian Stuart and the rest of the RPS management team for entrusting me to coach this project and allowing us to spread the word about what we've been doing.

All project participants for putting their hearts into this project and helping to drive the change process. I was amazed by the skill, creativity, and energy of this project team!

Mary and Tom Poppendieck for years of personal mentorship and cotraining in Lean software development and for encouraging me to write this book.

They also kindly contributed most of the content in Section 17.2, *Lean in a Nutshell*, on page 106.

My editor, Kay Keppler. I've never worked with an editor before, and I was surprised about how valuable this was. Kay not only improved the book, she helped me become a better writer!

All reviewers: Gunnar Ahlberg, Kevin Beam, Kent Beck, Pawel Brodzinski, Ward Cunningham, Doug Daniels, Chad Dumler-Montplaisir, Yves Hanoulle, Michael Hunter, Andy Keffalas, Maurice Kelly, Sebastian Lang, Rasmus Larsson, Mary Poppendieck, Sam Rose, Daniel Teng, Nancy Van Schooender-woert, Joshua White, and Colin Yates.

Martie Smith and Emma Mattsson for donating some great photographs.

Finally, my wife, Sophia, for granting me focus and flow (not easy with four small kids in the house...) so that I could finish the first draft of this book within days instead of months.

Henrik Kniberg
mailto:henrik.kniberg@crisp.se
Stockholm, October 2011

Part I

How We Work

Let's climb into the trenches and take a look at what this project is about and how things get done.

CHAPTER 1

About the Project

RPS ("rikspolisstyrelsen") is the Swedish national police authority, and the product we have built is a new digital investigation system called PUST ("Polisens mobila Utrednings STöd"). The basic idea is to equip every police car with a small laptop, a mobile Internet connection, and a web application that allows officers to handle all the investigation work quickly.

Suppose an officer catches a drunk driver. In the past, the officer would have had to capture all the information on paper, drive to the station, file a report, and then hand the case over to another investigator for further work. This would take a month or so.

With PUST, the officer captures all the information directly on the laptop, which is online and integrated directly with all relevant systems. The case is closed within a few days or even hours.

The system was rolled out nationwide in April 2011 and garnered quite a lot of media attention. The product has been featured in major newspapers, on TV, and on the radio, and so far the response has been very positive.[1]

Petty crimes are now processed, on average, six times faster,[2] and the police can spend more time in the field and less time at the station. More crimes can be resolved and with higher quality, which is likely to improve crime statistics over the long term. Staying in the field is also more motivating for the officers. Police like to do police work, not paperwork!

Furthermore, the project itself has gone well. We've had surprisingly few support issues and bug reports, compared to past projects of similar complexity and scale. PUST is a complicated system because it has to do the following:

- Integrate with a huge number of legacy systems

- Be very user friendly since police will be using the system in real time while doing interrogations

- Be highly secure

- Comply with a lot of complicated laws and regulations

This project was very important to RPS. In fact, the Minister for Justice had declared publicly that the primary focus of the Swedish police was to become more effective and reduce the processing time for investigations. The high stakes, complex technology, and aggressive timeline made it clear that we probably couldn't pull off this project using traditional methods. We were therefore allowed to explore new and more effective ways of working, which is what this book is about.

---

1. www.dn.se/nyheter/sverige/polisen-utreder-betydligt-snabbare-med-ny-metod

2. www.polisen.se/sv/Aktuellt/Nyheter/Gemensam/2011/april-juni/Snabbare-brottsutredningar-med-PUST/

PUST is part of a cultural change within RPS, a nationwide Lean initiative throughout the whole organization. So, it made a lot of sense to start applying Lean principles to the development process itself too!

1.1 Timeline

The goal of the project was to make the PUST system available to all police in Sweden by early 2011. Development started around September 2009. The first release to production (a pilot) happened one year later, followed by a series of bimonthly follow-up releases.

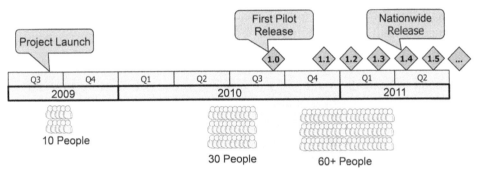

The project size was initially about ten people in Q3 2009, scaled to about thirty people in mid-2010, and then doubled to sixty-plus people in Q4 2010.

The key milestones were 1.0 (the first pilot release to real users) and 1.4 (the nationwide release). The system will, of course, continue to evolve over many years, so 1.4 is by no means the last release.

One year to first release might seem like a long time to Agile folks, but compared to other government projects of similar scope and complexity, this was extremely short! Some of these types of projects have taken up to seven years until first release! Release to production every second month is also quite an unusual concept. Many government organizations release only once or twice per year. We're hoping to reduce this even further to a monthly release cycle.

All these factors—the short release cycles and the aggressive scaling—drove the need to evolve the organization and development process quickly.

And that's how I got involved as coach.

I was on the project from December 2010 to June 2011, working roughly two to three days per week. My main focus was on putting Lean and Agile principles into practice and helping the teams evolve just the right process for their context. That's what the rest of this book is about—what we did, what

Joe asks:
Why Release Often? Isn't That Expensive?

Well, yes, each release does carry a fixed cost. But the release is the *moment of truth* —the only time that we really learn about how our product fits the user's needs! The longer we wait between releases, the more bugs and incorrect assumptions we will embed in the code. Also, with smaller and more frequent releases, the pain and risk for each release is reduced.

problems we encountered, how we dealt with them, and what we learned. It was a challenging but fun journey!

One thing to keep in mind, though...

This book is basically a snapshot of how our process looked in June 2011. One of the most important characteristics of a Lean process is that it *keeps evolving*. Sometimes we find better solutions. Sometimes a seemingly great solution yesterday causes a new problem today. Sometimes our environment and circumstances change, forcing us to adapt.

So, by the time you read this book, the project may well look very different.

1.2 How We Sliced the Elephant

The key to minimizing risk in large projects is to find a way to "slice the elephant," that is, find a way to release the system in small increments instead of saving up for a big-bang release at the end. Ideally, each increment should independently add value to the users and knowledge to the teams.

We sliced this elephant across two dimensions: geographic location and type of crime.

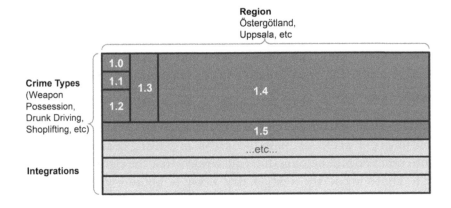

- *Release 1.0-1.2*: Pilot releases to only one region—Östergötland—supporting only a small number of common crime types such as drunk driving and weapon possession. Other crime types were handled the old manual way. For each subsequent release we improved the stability and added more crime types.

- *Release 1.3*: Expanded the release to a second region—Uppsala.

- *Release 1.4*: Expanded the release to the rest of Sweden. This was the "main" release.

- *Release 1.5*: Additional crime types added, with new integrations to various systems such as tracking of confiscated goods.

In addition to the bimonthly feature releases, we made small "patch" releases every few weeks to provide bug fixes and minor improvements to existing functionality.

1.3 How We Involved the Customer

PUST was an in-house project; the customer, users, and developers were all part of the Swedish police organization.

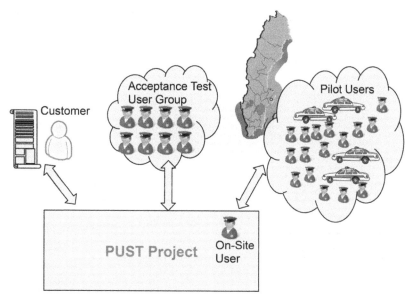

One person acted as the main "customer" (or "buyer") to the project. She had a list of features at a pretty high level. We called them *feature areas*, which roughly equates to what agile folks would call *epics*. This list was used for high-level scheduling and release planning.

In addition to the customer, there was an *on-site user* in the building with the development teams. The on-site users were there to give detailed feedback, see demos, answer questions from developers, and so on. Initially we had on-site users only once per week or so, but during later stages we had on-site users almost every day, through a rotating schedule.

A week before each release we had an *acceptance test group* come in, typically ten or so police officers, investigators, and other real users. This group would spend a couple of days trying the latest release candidate and giving feedback. Usually the system worked quite well by the time it reached acceptance test, so we rarely had any nasty surprises coming up at that point.

As soon as the first release was out the door, we had a group of *pilot users* in Östergötland (a region in southern part of Sweden) hard at work, giving us a continuous stream of feedback on our efforts.

CHAPTER 2

Structuring the Teams

One of the key challenges in software projects is how to organize people into decently sized teams and then how to coordinate between multiple teams.

As we scaled from thirty to sixty-plus people, we started running into serious communication and coordination difficulties—typical symptoms of growth pain. Fortunately, we were all located on the same floor; everybody in the project was within at most thirty seconds' walking distance from each other. As a result, we could quite easily experiment with how to organize the project. In fact, collocation may well have been the most important success factor of this project.

We gradually evolved the team structure to something like this:

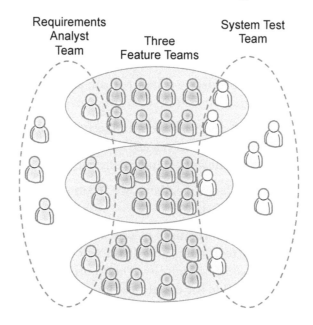

We have five teams: one requirements team, three feature development teams, and one system test team. Some people are outside of the team structure to handle specialist functions and coordination functions. This includes the project manager, project administrator, configuration manager, e-learning specialist, performance test expert, development manager, coach, and so on.

The three feature teams are basically Scrum teams; that is, each team is collocated, cross-functional, self-organized, and capable of developing and testing a whole feature. For more info on Scrum, see Section 17.3, *Scrum in a Nutshell*, on page 109.

The requirements analyst team is essentially a virtual team, so instead of sitting together as a team, they are spread around to ensure that everyone on the project has close access to a requirements analyst. Within this team are essentially three subroles:

- Some analysts are embedded in one of the feature teams and follow that team's features all the way through development into test, answering questions and clarifying the requirements along the way.

- Some analysts focus on the "big picture" and aren't embedded in any feature team. They look further into the future to define high-level feature areas.

- The rest of the members of the analyst team are flexible and move between the two other subroles depending on where they are needed most at the moment.

The test team follows a similar virtual team structure, with corresponding subroles:

- Some testers are embedded in a feature team and help that team get their software tested and debugged at a feature level.

- Some testers are "big-picture" testers and focus on doing high-level system tests and integration tests on release candidates as they come out. The person coordinating that work is informally called the *system test general.*

- The rest of the test team members are flexible and move between the other two roles as needed.

In the past, the teams were organized by specialty. We had a distinct requirements team, a distinct test team, and distinct development teams that did not have embedded testers or analysts. That didn't scale very well, because as more people were added to the project, communication problems developed. Teams tended to communicate with other teams through documents rather than talking, and they tended to blame problems on each other. Teams also tended to focus on getting their part of the work done instead of the whole product. For example, a requirements analyst would consider his work for a feature "done" when the requirements document had been written and signed off, instead of staying with that feature all the way through to production.

The level of collaboration improved dramatically as we evolved to a more Scrum-like structure, with cross-functional teams of analysts, testers, and developers sitting together. We didn't go "all the way," though; we kept some analysts and testers outside of the feature teams so they could focus on the "big picture" instead of individual features. This scaled quite nicely and gave us a good balance between short-term feature focus and long-term product focus.

CHAPTER 3

Attending the Daily Cocktail Party

If you walk into this project on any day before 10:15 a.m., it will feel like walking into a cocktail party! People are everywhere, standing in small groups and communicating.

You'll see groups standing in semicircles in front of boards, engaged in conversation, and moving sticky notes around. You'll see people moving between teams, debates going on, and decisions being made. Suddenly a group will break apart, and some individuals will move to another group to continue the conversation. New groups sometimes form in the hall to follow up on some side conversation.

By 10:15 the daily cocktail party is over, and most people are back at their desks.

This may look chaotic at first glance, but in fact, it's highly structured.

3.1 First Tier: Feature Team Daily Stand-up

First up are the feature team daily stand-ups.

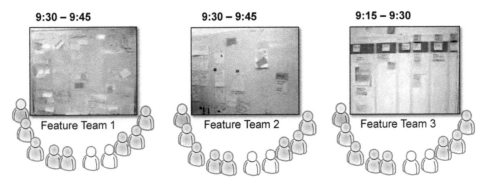

Two of the teams meet at 9:30, and one of the team meets at 9:15 (each team decides their own meeting time). Everyone on the team stands up in a rough semicircle in front of their task board, discussing the work they are going to do today and any problems and issues that need to be addressed.

> **Sally:** *I'm going to chase that darned memory leak today.*
>
> **Jeff:** *You probably need to upgrade the profiler tool first. I had problems with that last week.*
>
> **Sally:** *OK, thanks for the heads-up. I'll come get you if I get stuck.*

Some teams use the Scrum formula (answering "What did I do yesterday," "What am I doing today," and "What is blocking me"), and others are more informal about it. These meetings usually take ten to fifteen minutes and are facilitated by a team leader (which equates pretty much to Scrum master).

3.2 Second Tier: Sync Meetings per Specialty

At precisely 9:45, a second set of daily stand-ups takes place, during which the members of each specialty (requirements analysis, test, development) meet separately to synchronize their work across all feature teams.

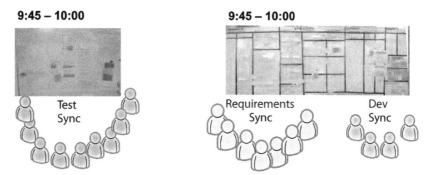

All the testers gather in front of a test status board and discuss how to make best use of their time today. The embedded testers have just completed the daily stand-up within their feature team, so they have fresh information about what is going on within each team.

> **Tom:** *Today we need to focus on usability issues in system test. Any help is appreciated.*

> **Lisa:** *I'll join you in an hour or so. My team is finishing a logging feature. After that, they can probably do without me for the rest of the day.*

At the same time, the requirements analysts are having their own sync meeting, including the embedded analysts who just came out of their feature team stand-up meeting with fresh information.

> **Jim:** *The folks on my team seem confused about the new usability guidelines.*

> **John:** *My team too!*

> **Maria:** *Oh, maybe that's why system test has become a bottleneck again. They seem to be struggling with inconsistent user interface design. Any proposals?*

> **Jim:** *Let's set up a workshop and discuss the new guidelines.*

> **Maria:** *OK, I'll bring up this at the project sync meeting right after this. We'll find a good time today and try to get at least one developer and tester from each team to join.*

At the same time, the team leads from each feature team, plus the development manager are having their *dev sync meeting*. The team leads just came out of their feature team stand-up meeting with fresh information.

> **Jeff:** *My team is finishing off the logging feature (points to a card on the wall). We'll probably get started with the database migration this afternoon.*
>
> **Sam:** *Wait, does that mean we need to update the build scripts?*
>
> **Jeff:** *Yeah. It's easy, though. Ask Lisa if you need help. At the team stand-up, she said she didn't have much to do today.*

The test sync meeting takes place in front of a test status board, while the requirements sync and dev sync meetings take place in front of the project board (see Chapter 4, *The Project Board*, on page 19). These three meetings take place in parallel just a few meters from each other, which makes it a bit noisy and chaotic, but the collaboration is very effective. If anybody from one team needs info from another, they can just walk over a few meters to the other meeting and ask a question.

Some people (such as the project manager and I) float around between the meetings, absorbing what is going on and trying to get a feel for which high-level issues need to be resolved. Sometimes we stay outside the meetings, and sometimes we get pulled into a discussion.

3.3 Third Tier: Project Sync Meeting

Finally, at precisely 10 a.m., the project sync meeting takes place in front of the project board.

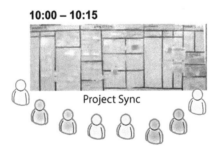

10:00 – 10:15

Project Sync

The people at this meeting are informally referred to as the *cross-team* (or *tvärgrupp* in Swedish)—a cross-section of the whole project. In our case, that equates to one person from each specialty and one person from each feature team, plus a few other folks such as the project manager, configuration manager, and myself.

The project sync meeting is where we look at the big picture, focusing on the flow of functionality from analysis to production: Which team is doing what today? What is blocking our flow right now? Where is the bottleneck, and how can we alleviate it? Where will the bottleneck be next? Are we on track with respect to the release plan? Does anybody not know what to do today?

This not only gives us a great bird's-eye perspective of what is going on, it lets us solve problems quickly, especially collaboration issues between teams. If "us" and "them" work together every day, then sooner or later "us" and "them" become just "us."

That's it. A total of seven stand-up meetings every day, organized into three layers. Each meeting is *timeboxed* to fifteen minutes, each meeting has a core set of participants who show every day, and each meeting is public, so anybody can visit any meeting if they want to learn what is going on or have something to contribute. And it's all over by 10:15 a.m.

If some important topic comes up during a daily and can't be resolved within fifteen minutes, we schedule a follow-up meeting with the people needed to resolve that issue. Some of the most interesting and valuable discussions take place right after the project sync meeting, as people stand in small clusters dealing with stuff that came up during the daily stand-ups.

This structure of daily meetings was something that we gradually evolved into. When we started doing the "daily cocktail party" (which, by the way, is my term, not an official term we use in the project), I was a bit concerned that people might think we were having too many meetings. That turned out not to be the case. On the contrary, the team members insist that these meetings are highly valuable, and I can see that the energy level is usually high and problems get solved.

Most people need to go to only one meeting. Some individuals need to go to two meetings. The team lead of a feature team goes to his team stand-up as well as the dev sync meeting. The embedded tester in a feature team goes to the team stand-up as well as the test sync meeting, and so on. This is a very effective way of "linking" communication channels and making sure that important knowledge, information, and decisions propagate quickly throughout the entire project.

Many problems that would otherwise result in the creation of documents and process rules are resolved directly at these morning meetings. One concrete example is deciding which team is to develop which feature; another example is deciding whether to spend our time developing customer-facing functionality today or spend it implementing customer-invisible improvements to the technical infrastructure. Instead of setting up policy rules for this, the teams simply talk about this during the daily meetings and make decisions on-the-fly based on the current situation. This is the key to staying agile in a big project and not getting bogged down in bureaucracy.

CHAPTER 4

The Project Board

The project board is the communication hub of the project. Ours is a several-meter-long whiteboard showing all key project features flowing through the pipeline from requirements, development, and system test, all the way into production.

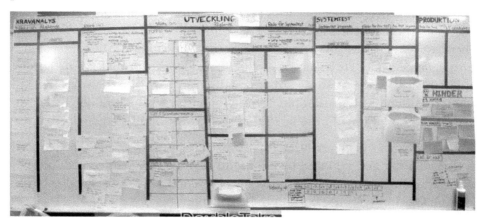

If you are into Kanban, you'll recognize this as a *Kanban system*, which means that we track the flow of value from idea to production and that we limit the amount of work in progress at each step of the process. For more on Kanban, see Section 17.5, *Kanban in a Nutshell*, on page 112.

Here's a summary of what the columns mean:

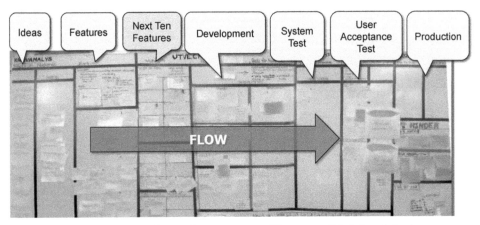

The leftmost column is where ideas come in. These are high level-feature areas. Each feature area is written down on an *epic* card. One example is "confiscation," which represents a whole series of features related to the confiscation of items from suspects.

The epic card sooner or later gets pulled into the second column (*analysis ongoing*), where it gets analyzed and split into user stories at a feature level. These are written down on *feature cards* in the third column. The third column corresponds roughly to a Scrum product backlog, except that it isn't strictly ordered. Most of the feature cards are written in user story format: "As X, I want Y so that Z." For example, "As investigator, I want to filter by region when I search for an address so that I can find the address quickly."

When an epic has been analyzed (that is, broken into features), the epic card is thrown away and replaced by a handful of more detailed feature cards in the third column. So, the epic cards never make it past the second column, and the feature cards are born in the third column.

Feature cards are the main "unit of currency" on the board.

The top ten features are selected and pulled into the "Next Ten Features" column. This usually happens at a biweekly meeting that corresponds roughly to a Scrum sprint planning meeting (we even call it that). See Chapter 13, *Planning the Sprint and Release*, on page 85 for more info on how the top ten are selected.

The three feature teams continuously pull cards from the "Next Ten Features" column into their own "Dev in Progress" column when they have capacity, and into the "Ready for System Test" column when the feature is developed and tested at a feature level.

The test team regularly flushes the "Ready for System Test" column and pulls all those cards into the "System Test in Progress" column (and creates a corresponding system test branch in the version control system; see Chapter 14, *How We Do Version Control*, on page 89). Once system test is done, the test team releases to an acceptance test environment, moves the cards to the "Ready for Acceptance Test" column, and then starts another round of system tests on whatever features have been completed since. This was a big cultural shift—the move from "big system test at the end of the release cycle" to "continuous system test" (but with some batching).

Every second month (roughly), a bunch of real users show up and spend a couple of days doing acceptance testing (basically just trying the system out and giving feedback), so we move the cards to "Acceptance Test in Progress." When they're done testing and any final bugs have been found and fixed, the cards move to "Ready for Production." Shortly thereafter (when the system has been released), they move to the last column, "In Production." The cards sit there for a few weeks (so we can celebrate that something got into production) but are then removed to make space for new cards flowing in.

To the casual observer glancing at the board, this system might look like a waterfall process: requirements analysis→development→system test→acceptance test→production. There's a big difference, though. In a waterfall model, the requirements are all completed before development starts, and development is completed before testing starts. In a Kanban system, these phases are all going on in parallel. While one set of features is being acceptance-tested by users, another set of features is being system tested, a third set of features is being developed, and a fourth set of features is being analyzed and broken into user stories. It's a continuous flow of value from idea to production.

Well, it's semicontinuous, I should say. In our case it's a more or less continuous flow of value from idea to "Ready for Acceptance Test." New features are released to production roughly every second month and acceptance-tested in conjunction with that, so features sit around in "Ready for Acceptance Test" for a few weeks. Although I hope we can improve this in the future, it's turned out to be not much of a problem. Since we have on-site users giving us feedback during development, we've found that by the time a feature reaches "Ready for Acceptance Test," it pretty much works as expected, and few serious problems are found after that stage.

> ### Using Kanban to Discover Scrum
>
> This seems to be a general pattern: I see many Kanban teams that gradually discover (or sometimes rediscover) the value of many of the Scrum practices. In fact, sometimes Kanban teams start doing Kanban because they didn't like Scrum and then later discover that Scrum was actually pretty good and their problems had been exposed by Scrum, not caused by it. Their real problem was that they had been doing Scrum too much "by the book" instead of inspecting and adapting it to their context.
>
> More on that in my other book *Kanban and Scrum: Making the Most of Both* [KS09].

4.1 Our Cadences

A *cadence* is something that happens over and over at regular intervals, forming a rhythm or heartbeat in the project. Here is a summary of our cadences:

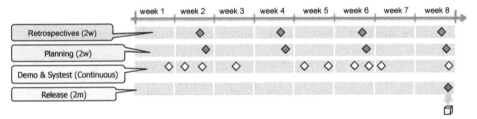

- Retrospectives happen every second week (every week for some teams). That's where we look for ways to improve the process.

- Planning happens every second week (approximately). That's where we decide which features to focus on next.

- Demo and system test is done in a continuous fashion, as features get done.

- Release to production is done approximately every second month

We've been evolving more and more toward a Scrum-like model. Initially, retrospectives were held twice as often as planning meetings; now they happen every second week, one day after each other. Demo and reviews are done continuously now, but we're considering doing a high-level product demo/review every second week. And guess what—doing retrospectives, planning, and demos together in the same cadence is basically the definition of a Scrum sprint.

This evolution toward a more Scrum-like model was not really intentional. It was just the result of a series of process improvements triggered by real-life problems.

4.2   How We Handle Urgent Issues and Impediments

A traffic system metaphor is very useful when dealing with Kanban boards. Think of the board as a series of roads, with each card representing a car trying to move across the board from left to right.

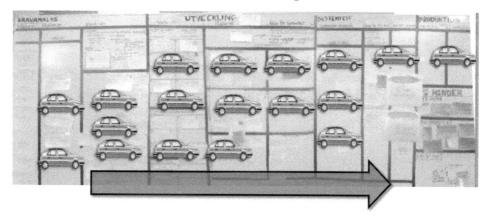

We want to optimize the flow; therefore, we *don't* want to fill up the board. We all know what happens to a traffic system when it is 100 percent full—the traffic system slows to a halt.

We need space, or *slack*, to absorb variation and enable fast flow.

Having slack in the system not only enables fast flow, it also enables escalation. On our board we use police car magnets (of course!) to mark items that are urgent and need special treatment to move through the system faster.

We also mark impediments ("road blocks") using pink stickies.

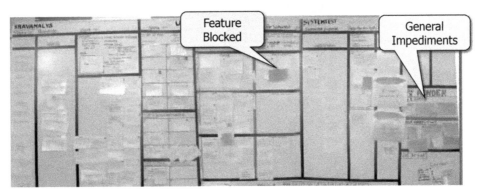

If a specific feature is blocked (for example, because we don't have access to a third-party system needed to test that feature), we put a pink sticky on that feature, describing the problem and the date that it started. A section on the right side—Top Three Impediments—also shows more general problems that aren't tied to any specific feature (such as a build environment not working).

At the daily meetings we focus on removing these blockers. Just as with a traffic system, a blocker that stays around for too long will cause ripple effects throughout the whole system. Plus, nothing will flow faster than the bottleneck section of the road, so we focus all efforts on resolving these bottlenecks.

Here's an example of a blocker being dealt with at the daily project sync meeting:

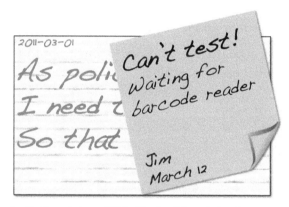

Eric: So, what's the status of this blocked item? Jim?

Jim: Still no barcode reader. It was supposed to be delivered last week; I have no idea when we will get it, so I can't really test my code.

Eric: Hmmm. Do we just wait and hold our breath, or is there anything else we can do?

Tracee: I worked with barcode readers in my last project; maybe we still have some lying around?

Jim: It's probably not the right model, but I can start testing on that. It's a start.

Eric: OK, and in the meantime I'll escalate the problem and put some heat on the supplier. Do you need anything else?

Jim: No, I think this is the best we can do for this issue for today.

The next day, if the problem hasn't been resolved, the pink sticky note will still be up there as a reminder to follow up on this issue. The date on the sticky indicates how long it has been up there, and the name indicates who is focusing on solving the issue (so we know who to ask about it).

Eric: I see the barcode issue is still up as a blocker....

Jim: Yeah. Tracee and I tried her reader, but it wasn't compatible so we couldn't test on it at all.

Eric: Too bad. Well, I talked to the supplier yesterday and couldn't get a clear commitment. I also talked to the customer and mentioned the problem. To my surprise, they said the barcode feature isn't really that important for this release and that we could skip it if it's causing trouble.

Jim: Great! Then I'll start working on another feature instead.

Eric: And I'll start looking for a new supplier, so we're ready when this feature pops up in the future.

The project board is probably the single most important communication artifact in the project. It provides a high-level picture of what is going on in the project and illustrates flow and bottlenecks in real time.

But how can a physical board like this work in practice with sixty-plus people on the project? Coming up next: scaling the Kanban boards.

CHAPTER 5

Scaling the Kanban Boards

The speed of a project is largely determined by how well everyone understands what's going on. If everyone knows where we are right now and where we're going, it's much easier for everyone to move in the same direction.

As we approached staff levels of sixty people, this became a challenge. Each team had its own team board showing what was going on within the team, covering which features are in progress and who's working on which task related to that feature. However, we were missing the big picture. What's going in the whole project? Where's the bottleneck right now? Which new features are coming down the pipeline? Which features will be finished in time for the release?

That's why we created the project board. It's a way to keep track of the big picture by showing project features as they move from requirements to development, to system test, and into production.

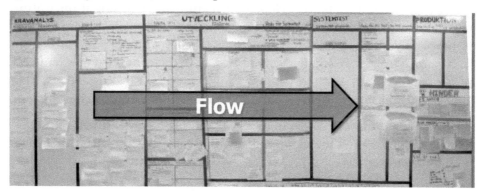

This board had a strong effect on the culture of the organization. Now we could *see*! And we all had the *same picture*!

The collaboration between teams improved dramatically since each team could see how their actions influenced (and sometimes disrupted) the overall flow of features into production.

However, we didn't want to remove the team boards, since they were great for visualizing the daily task-level work going on within each team and helping team members stay in sync with each other. And we didn't want to put all that detailed team-local information on the project board; it would get too cluttered, and we would lose the overview. So, we decided to have a two-layer system of boards—one shared project board plus three team boards.

The development columns on the project board were split into three horizontal swim lanes, one for each feature team:

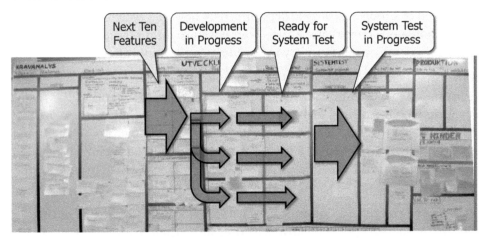

Each feature flows from "Next Ten Features" into one of the three feature teams. When that team has developed the feature and tested it at the feature level, it goes to "Ready for System Test." When the system test team finishes its previously ongoing round of system tests, they pull all new cards from each feature team's "Ready for System Test" into the combined "System Test in Progress" column and start a new round of system testing. See Section 9.1, *Continuous System Test*, on page 45 for more information on how we test.

Whenever a feature team pulls in a card from "Next Ten Features" to "Development in Progress," they clone that feature card and put it on their own team-internal board.

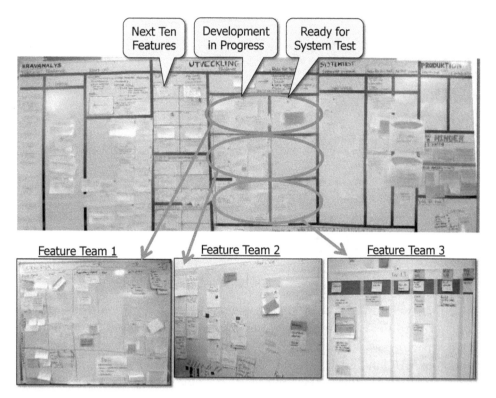

The feature team then breaks the work into tasks and writes those down as sticky notes tied to that feature. This is typically done in conjunction with an *analysis meeting*, where requirements analysts, testers, and developers collaborate to sketch out the design of this feature and identify the key tasks involved. Each task normally starts with a concrete verb, for example "write the GUI code" or "set up the DB tables" or "design the protocol."

So, the project board contains feature cards, and each feature team has their own board with the features they are working on plus the associated task breakdown. Imagine that you "double-click" a feature on the project board and "zoom in" to the corresponding team board to see which tasks are involved in that feature and who is working on what task.

Most feature teams also have avatar magnets to indicate who is working on which task. Your avatar says everything about your personality…

As you can see in the pictures, each team has their own board layout. We have not tried to standardize this. Instead, we let each team find whatever board structure works best for them. Most teams do have work-in-progress limits (see WIP limits; Chapter 11, *Managing Work in Progress*, on page 65) and a definition of "done" (see Chapter 7, *Defining Ready and Done*, on page 35) and avatar magnets on their boards.

This two-tier system of physical Kanban boards turned out to work very well, although there was some initial confusion about how to keep everything in sync. It's clear that the boards have become a point of gravity in the project; teams naturally gather around their board whenever they need to synchronize work or solve problems. Most team members focus on their team-level board, while team leads and managers focus on both the team-level board and the project-level board.

As time passes, more and more team members have started showing interest in the project-level board, which is a good indicator that people are focusing on the big picture rather than just on their own work.

However, if we *really* want people to focus, we need something more: a clearly defined high-level goal.

CHAPTER 6

Tracking the High-Level Goal

People are more likely to focus on the high-level goal if they know what it is.

I know, that sounds rather obvious. But yet in many organizations I've worked with, managers *think* that everyone knows the high-level goal, and then it turns out that each person has a different answer when we ask them what that goal is.

Our high-level project goal is usually posted right on the Kanban board. For example, during Q1 2011 we had the goal "Deliver on April 5 a version with no important defects that is releasable to the whole country." A milestone along that path was to deliver to two new regions on March 14.

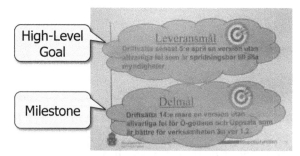

When we reach a goal, we write a new goal statement for the next release. The goal statement acts as a guiding light. Sometimes we need to make difficult trade-offs, and having a clear, high-level goal helps everyone stay in sync about what's important for the next release.

Once every week or two we do a reality check. Typically the project manager asks at the project sync meeting, "Do you believe we'll reach this goal?" Everybody writes down a number from one to five (sometimes we just hold up fingers).

- 5 = Definitely

- 4 = Probably

- 3 = Barely

- 2 = Probably not

- 1 = Forget it

Here's an example:

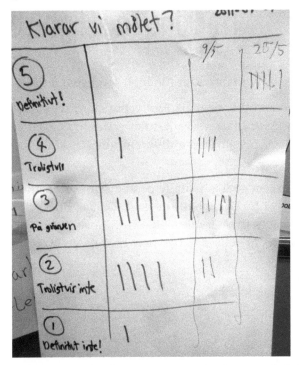

This chart shows three rounds of votes. During the first week (leftmost column of votes), there was low confidence in the goal; the next week, confidence increased; and the week after that, it was all 5s!

Whenever we start seeing 2s and 1s, we reevaluate the goal and discuss what needs to change to improve our confidence. These are typical actions:

- Remove an impediment ("Let's buy a new build server to replace the broken one!")

- Help a bottleneck ("Let's all do testing today!")

- Reduce scope ("If we remove feature X from this release, we can still reach the goal!")

- Adjust the goal ("This goal is no longer realistic; let's define a new goal that we actually believe in!")

- Work harder ("Who can come in on Saturday?")

Any of the first four are preferable to the last, since the root cause of the problem is usually not that we aren't working hard. In fact, sometimes the root cause of the problem is that we are working *too* hard and not taking time to think.

The votes are mostly based on gut feel but also to a certain extent on visible information, including the cards on the board, metrics such as cycle time and velocity (see Chapter 12, *Capturing and Using Process Metrics*, on page 73), and charts such as this feature burn-up:

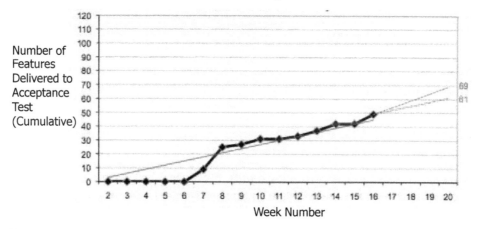

The x-axis shows the week, and the y-axis shows the total number of features that have been completed by that week. This is a nice visualization of the system growing over time.

The two dotted lines poking out to the right are trend lines, showing one optimistic and one pessimistic projection of how many features will be finished in time for the next release. We're still just guessing, of course, but the guesses are based on empirical data and not just, well, guesses.

Armed with this data, we can make a simple and realistic release plan that doesn't try to hide the uncertainty:

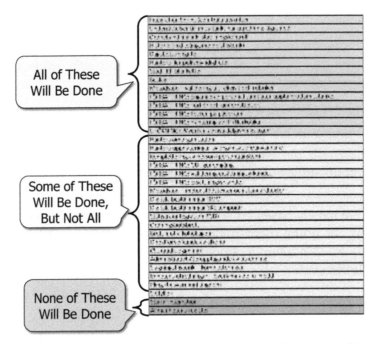

As we get closer to the release date, we get more and more confident about which features will be done and which won't, so the uncertainty (the middle section) decreases.

By the way, we don't use any fancy project management tool to generate these charts. We use a simple spreadsheet.

Anyway, this type of continuous reality check is a very simple and useful technique to detect and avoid death marches (projects where everyone knows they're going to fail but still keep marching dutifully). If people can agree on a goal that they believe in, this has an immensely positive effect on self-organization and collaboration. Conversely, if people don't understand the goal or don't believe the goal is achievable, they will unconsciously disassociate themselves from the business goal and focus on personal goals such as "have fun coding" or "just get my part of the work done and go home."

I can strongly recommend having a clear goal and periodic reality check, no matter what type of project you are involved in. The cost of doing this is very low, and the benefit is very high!

Defining Ready and Done

It's important to be very clear about what the columns on the board mean. Especially in big projects, the more people involved, the greater the risk of confusion, and the greater the *cost* of confusion.

The blue text at the top of most columns on our project board is the *definition of done* for that column (which also means *definition of ready* for the subsequent column). The two most important definitions for us are *definition of ready for development* and *definition of ready for system test*, since that's where we used to have the most problems.

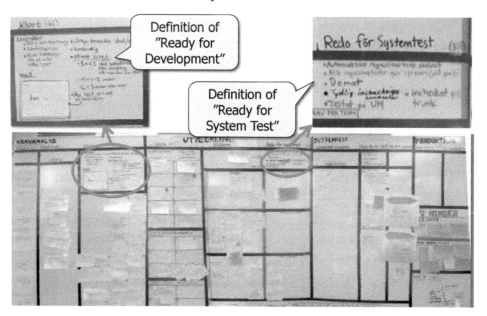

7.1 Ready for Development

The "Ready for Development" column essentially means "Here's a bunch of features that we've broken down and estimated and clarified, but we haven't yet decided which of these we are going to develop and in which order." So, this corresponds roughly to a Scrum product backlog. For a feature to be ready for development, it must have the following characteristics:

- It must have an *ID*. The ID is used as a key when you're looking up more information about this feature, in case there are any associated use case specifications or other documents. These documents are accessible on the project wiki by clicking the corresponding ID.

- It must have a *contact person*. The contact person is typically the requirements analyst who has the most domain knowledge about this feature.

- It must be *valuable* to customers. When breaking down epics into deliverable stories, we want to make sure we haven't lost the customer value along the way. The requirements analysts have the final say on this matter.

- It must be *estimated* by the team. The estimates are normally done by a small group consisting of a tester, a developer, and a requirements analyst playing Planning Poker (see Chapter 19, *Sizing the Backlog with Planning Poker*, on page 125). We use T-shirt sizes (small, medium, large). These are size estimates, not time estimates. But to make the estimation process easier, we use this as a rough guideline:

  - *Small* means "Under perfect conditions this will take less than one week of elapsed time to get to 'Ready For Acceptance Test.'" *Perfect conditions* means that we have exactly the right people working only on this feature with no disruptions.

  - *Medium* means one to two weeks (again, under perfect conditions).

  - *Large* means more than two weeks. Large features have to be broken down further before they are allowed into development.

- It must have an *acceptance test* scenario written on the backside of the card. This is a concrete set of steps describing the most typical test scenario. Here's an example:

  "Joe Cop logs in, looks up case #235, and closes it. He then looks up case #235 again and sees that it's closed."

7.2   Ready for System Test

"Ready for System Test" means that the feature team has done everything they can think of to ensure that this feature works and doesn't have any important defects. They have, however, focused on testing the feature itself, not the whole release that it would be part of.

For a long time system test was a bottleneck, and one of the major reasons for that was the high number of unnecessary defects passing into system test. By "unnecessary defects," I mean feature-level defects that could have been found way before putting it all together into a system test. So, our *definition of ready for system test* is there to keep the quality bar high and catch those pesky bugs early. It's also there to give the feature team a sense of responsibility for quality and to give them permission to spend the necessary time to ensure that a feature really works, before delivering it to system test and moving on to the next feature.

So, here is our *definition of ready for system test*:

- *Acceptance test automated*: This means that some kind of end-to-end feature-level acceptance test or integration test has been automated. We used to use Selenium for that (which runs tests directly against the web interface), but we eventually moved to Concordion. The Selenium tests were just too brittle for our Ajax-riddled web interface, and Concordion fit better with our move toward Specification By Example.[1]

- *Regression tests pass*: All automated tests for previously existing features pass. Sometimes a new feature breaks an old feature, so we have to make sure that all old tests are run on a regular basis.

- *Demonstrated*: The team has demonstrated this feature to the rest of the team, the on-site user, the requirements analyst, the system tester, and the usability expert. This helps us catch usability issues *early* so they don't show up in system test or (even worse) user acceptance test.

- *Clear check-in comments*: When checking in code related to this feature, the check-in comment should be tagged with the ID of this feature, plus an easily understandable comment about what was done. This provides a minimum level of traceability (big projects always seem to fuss about traceability...).

---

1.   www.specificationbyexample.com

- *Tested in the development environment*: Each team has a dedicated test environment, and this feature should be tested there (to avoid the "Hey, it works on *my* machine" syndrome).

- *Merged to trunk*: Code for this feature should be on the trunk, and any merge conflicts should be resolved. This is the basis of the stable trunk model we use (see Chapter 14, *How We Do Version Control*, on page 89).

7.3 How This Improved Collaboration

These two policy statements—*definition of ready for development* and *definition of ready for system test*—have significantly improved collaboration between the teams. This improvement stood out clearly when I did a short survey to check what people thought about all the process changes so far.

In the past, when we just started doing Kanban, each specialty team focused mostly on "their" part of the project board. The requirements analysts looked only at the left part of the project board and considered themselves "done" with a feature when a requirements document had been written. The developers looked only at the middle of the board, and the testers looked only at the right. The testers weren't involved in writing the requirements, so once a feature reached test, there was often confusion about how it was supposed to work. People spent a lot of effort arguing about the level of detail needed in the requirements documents.

These were just old habits. But the project board helped everyone *see* the problem, which is the first and most critical step toward solving it!

The collaboration problems gradually disappeared (well, significantly declined at least) within a few weeks after everyone had agreed on the definitions. The *definition of ready for development* can be achieved only if all specialties work together to estimate features, to break them into small enough deliverables without losing too much customer value, and to agree on acceptance tests.

Similarly, the *definition of ready for system test* can be achieved only if all specialties work together to run feature-level tests (both automated tests and manual exploratory tests) to determine whether this feature is good enough to release.

This clear need for continuous collaboration is what made the test team and requirements team agree to "lend" specialists to each feature team, thus making each feature team truly cross-functional (and *much* more effective)!

In general, writing a *definition of ready* at the top of each key column is one of those simple techniques that is useful in any kind of Kanban system.

CHAPTER 8

Handling Tech Stories

Tech stories are things that need to get done but that are uninteresting to the customer, such as upgrading a database, cleaning out unused code, refactoring a messy design, or catching up on test automation for old features. We call these *internal improvements*, but in retrospect, *tech stories* is probably a better term, since we're talking about stuff to be done with the product, not process improvements.

Tech stories are born in the "Ready for Development" section of the project board and enter development through a "Next Five Tech Stories" section (right below "Next Ten Features"). These are essentially two parallel input queues to development.

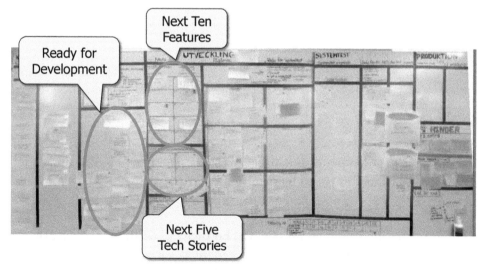

As you can see, there are quite a lot of cards under "Ready for Development," a mixed bag of features and tech stories. We don't waste time trying to put all those in priority order. Instead, we do a form of "just in time" prioritization by continuously identifying the next ten features and next five tech stories. This provides just enough of a work buffer to keep the feature teams from running out of things to work on.

When a feature team has capacity to start something new, they either pull a feature from "Next Ten Features" or pull a tech story from "Next Five Tech Stories." We have no static rule defining the correct balance between these two. Instead, we continuously discuss and adjust the balance during the daily stand-up meetings.

Tech stories are distinguished from features by a green spot in the corner of the card. This lets us distinguish between the two even after they have been pulled into development, so the project board reveals how we are balancing our time between features and tech stories.

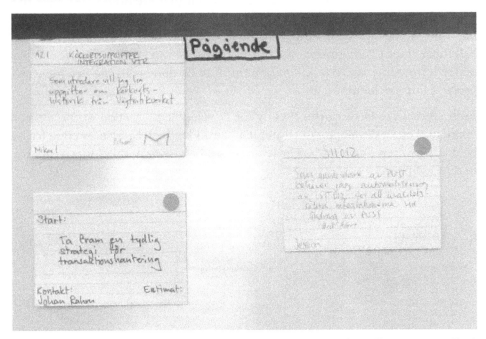

Usually features dominate, but here are some examples of situations that caused us to focus mostly on tech stories for a while:

8.1   Example 1: System Test Bottleneck

System testing had become an obvious bottleneck, so there was clearly no point developing new features and adding to the bottleneck. Once this became clear, the developers focused on implementing tech stories that would make system test easier—mostly test automation stuff. In fact, the test manager was tasked with creating a *test automation backlog*, prioritizing it, and feeding it to the developers via "Top Five Tech Stories." The testers became customers!

For more information on this technique, see Chapter 18, *Reducing the Test Automation Backlog*, on page 117.

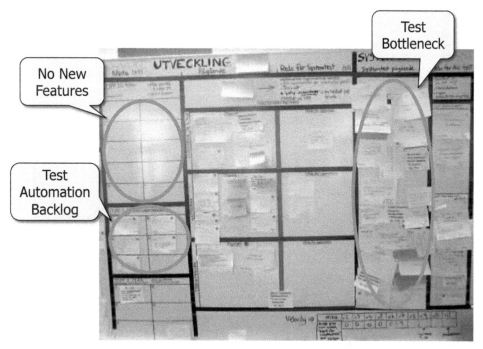

8.2 Example 2: Day Before the Release

It was the day before a major release, and the team wanted to get that release out the door before starting a bunch of new features. So, they focused on last-minute bug fixing. If they didn't have any bugs to fix at the moment, they worked on tech stories—typically things that we had wanted to do for a long time but had never gotten around to, such as removing unused code, catching up on refactoring, and learning new tools.

As you see from the board, lots of tech stories (green spots) are in progress.

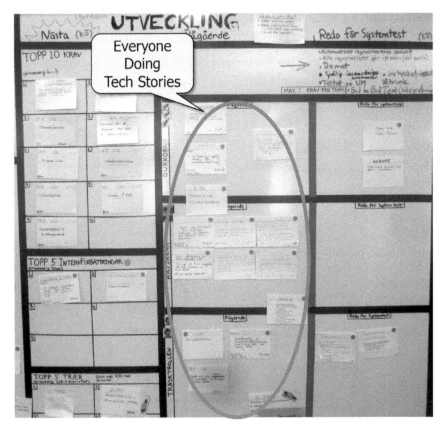

8.3   Example 3: The 7-Meter Class

Here's a cool way to make a business case for a tech story. One of the classes in our code base was getting way out of control and needed some significant refactoring, but there was some resistance to spending time on that. So, one of the team leads *printed out the whole class* and laid it across the conference table! It was more than 7 meters long (23 feet)!

Looking at that monstrous printout, everyone clearly saw that we needed a tech story to fix that class immediately! No argument needed. This also illustrated the consequence of being in a hurry and not paying enough attention to design.

We had some fun speculating about future developments along this theme. How about if we estimate features in code-meters and measure velocity in code-meters per day? We could even separate *ideal* code-meters (how long the code would be if we kept it really clean), with *actual* code-meters. Subtract those two, and you get technical debt—in meters! We could even draw a line in the floor to symbolize how much technical debt we have ("Hey look, we

On a Side Note...

I've never seen a project of this scale with so little *drama* in conjunction with releases! Almost disappointing....

Where is the customary panic and rush and all-night crunching the day before the release? Where is the subsequent onslaught of support issues and panicky hot fixing the day after the release? I came in the day after the most important release (the nationwide release that was the focal point of the whole project), and there was barely any sign that anything significant had happened.

The reason for this was that the releases were well-rehearsed, because of the setup with on-site users and pilot releases. Of course, we'd had some problems with the earlier pilot releases—but that's why we do pilots, right?

Anyway, remember to celebrate releases—even when you get good at it and they're not as exciting anymore.

have 23 meters of debt!"). Or maybe we would have to use code-miles for that....

Um, OK, I'll stop now.

Anyway, now that we've started talking about code quality, let's talk about bugs.

CHAPTER 9

Handling Bugs

Before we moved to Kanban, we handled bugs the traditional way. The testers would find bugs during system test at the end of the development cycle and log them in the bug tracker. The bug tracker contained hundreds of bugs, and a change control board met every week to analyze, prioritize, and assign bugs to developers. This was a pretty boring and ineffective process for everyone involved (and everyone *was* involved...).

9.1 Continuous System Test

The Kanban system helped us see that we needed to do system test continuously (well, regularly at least), instead of saving it until the end. The test team resisted this initially, since system test takes time and it felt inefficient to do it more than once in the release cycle. But that is an illusion. It may *seem* more effective to do test only at the end, but if we include bug-fixing time in the equation, it is significantly *less* effective.

Here's what testing at the end typically looks like in a two-month release cycle:

And here is what it typically looks like if we do it more often:

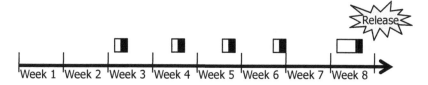

We can't test the *whole* system until the end, since the system isn't done until then. But we can still run partial system tests much earlier, based on whatever features are done at the time. And we can still do a full system test at the end. That final system test may take as long as before, but the bug-fixing time is dramatically reduced—and that's the big part! The bug-fixing time is reduced because we've already found and fixed many of the bugs earlier and because the bugs we do find at the end will tend to be newer bugs and therefore easier for the developers to find and fix. We also accelerate learning by finding bugs early.

So, let's put these two pictures together and graphically compare the testing and fixing time in both scenarios:

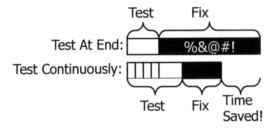

This is a very important picture. Look at it again, especially if you are a tester. Yes, your testing time increases in the second scenario. But the *total time* decreases!

Of course, another key element in this is test automation. We can never automate away *all* testing, but since we are doing system test over and over again, we want to automate *as much as we possibly can*!

9.2 Fix the Bugs Immediately!

Now when testers find a bug, they don't log it in the bug tracker. Instead, they write it down on a pink sticky note (like any other impediment) and go talk to the developers. In most cases, they know roughly who to go to, since each team has an embedded tester who works with the developers every day. Otherwise, they ask the team leads and find the right person to fix the bug (typically someone who has been working in that part of the code).

The developer and tester sit together and fix the bug on the spot, or the developer fixes the bug on his own and then gets back to the tester immediately. The point is, no more handoffs, no more delays, and no more communicating through the bug tracker. This is more effective for many reasons:

- Finding and fixing bugs earlier is more effective than finding and fixing bugs later.

> **Joe asks:**
> ## Do You Really Just *Ignore* Bugs That Don't Make Top Thirty?
>
> Well, OK, we sometimes log it in the bug tracker with status *deferred*, which is the equivalent of saying "Yes, we know about this but probably won't get around to fixing it." We do this mostly because it hurts a tester's soul to find a bug and then just ignore it. Even though it probably will never be fixed, most people seem to feel some sort of psychological comfort in writing it down. Plus it might be useful for data mining purposes—for example, to generate statistics showing which parts of the system are most bug-riddled.
>
> But basically, *deferred* bugs are outside of the top-thirty list, so *deferred* is for all practical purposes equivalent to a garbage can or a basement full of stuff that we don't need but don't have the heart to throw away right now.

- Face-to-face communication is more effective than written communication (because of the higher bandwidth).

- Everybody learns more, as developers and testers learn about each other's work.

- Less time is wasted managing long lists of old bugs.

Sometimes a bug is not important enough to fix immediately—for example, if it is only a minor annoyance to the users and implementing other features is more important than fixing this minor annoyance. In this case, well, yes, the tester will log the bug in the bug tracker. Unless it's full, of course.

What? Full? How can a bug tracker get full?

9.3 Why We Limit the Number of Bugs in the Bug Tracker

Before we moved to Kanban, we had hundreds of issues in the bug tracker. Now we have a hard limit of thirty.

If a bug is found, the first question is "Is this a blocker?" *Blocker* in this case means "The feature won't be releasable with this bug" or "This bug is more important to fix than building additional features." Write it on a pink sticky note and fix it now, like any other impediment. Don't put it in a queue.

If the bug is *not* a blocker, however, we have a decision to make: "Is this bug more important than any of the other top thirty bugs in the bug tracker?" If so, then that other bug is removed from the top thirty list to make room for this one. If not, then we ignore the new bug.

That way, the bug tracker continuously keeps us focused on the most important bugs and doesn't become an administrative burden.

Here's a summary of the workflow:

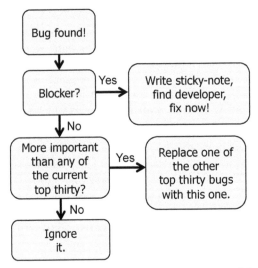

By limiting the size of the bug database, we no longer need long, boring change control board meetings to manage looooong lists of bugs that will probably never be fixed. The meetings still happen, but they're much shorter and more effective since they focus only on the edge cases—bugs that need to be discussed before they can be prioritized.

9.4 Visualizing Bugs

Of the top thirty bugs, we also identify the top five. Those go up on cards on the project board. So, that's a third input queue to development. "Next Ten Features," "Next Five Tech Stories," and "Next Five Bugs."

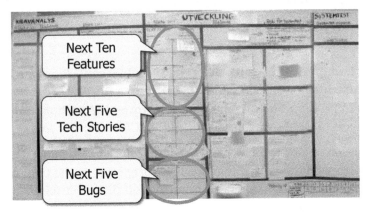

Bugs cards are written with red marker, so they are easily distinguished from features and tech stories.

The bugs that come in through the "Next Five Bugs" queue were not important enough to be a pink sticky note and get fixed immediately but were important enough to go on the "Next Five Bugs" list (typically after spending some time in the top thirty list in the bug tracker). So, it will be fixed soon, but just not at this moment.

When the team has capacity (typically right after finishing a feature), they will discuss whether to grab one of the next ten features, one of the next five tech stories, or one of next five bugs.

Limiting the size of the bug tracker builds trust. The bug list is short, but the stuff in there actually *does get fixed*, rather than sitting around for months without anything happening. If a bug is unlikely to be fixed (because it didn't make top thirty), we are honest about that from start, instead of building up false expectations.

That's the idea. Or something like that.

One improvement area we still face is that we still haven't found a clean, consistent way to visualize bugs. We're still experimenting a lot with this. The testers like to have a clear picture of which bugs are currently being fixed, so they have set up a separate board for this. The advantage of that system has to be balanced against the disadvantage of having yet another board to keep track of. Where does the bug sticky note go—on the bug board, the project board, or the team board? Or should we be duplicating bug sticky notes? What about really small bugs, things that just take a few minutes to fix, how do we avoid creating too much administrative overhead for these? Lots of questions, lots of experimentation....

So, basically we've come a long way and found a solution that enables us to find and fix bugs quickly, improve collaboration between developers and testers, avoid collecting long lists of stale bugs in the bug tracker, and avoid long boring change control board meetings. But we're still trying to figure out the visualization issue and experimenting with how to get just the right level of detail on the boards.

9.5 Preventing Recurring Bugs

Some types of bugs keep coming back. Often they're simple things, such as labels in the user interface being misaligned or misspelled. The important question is how the bugs get into the system in the first place—what underlying process problem is causing the technical problem?

To aid in fixing this problem (instead of just complaining about it), the testers have a section on their board called *recurring bugs*. Remember that I said bugs are written on pink stickies and treated like any impediment? Well, when the testers feel that a specific bug gives them a strong feeling of déjà vu, they post that under *recurring bugs* on their board. This is limited to a handful.

(You've noticed the theme by now, right? Limit all queues!)

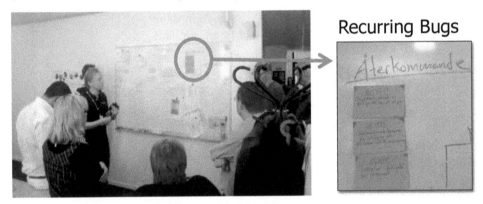

Once in a while one of the feature teams will have a defect prevention meeting, where they take one of the recurring bugs and do a root-cause analysis. How did that bug get into the code? What *systemic problems* are causing us to repeatedly create this type of bug, and what can we do about it? Sometimes it has to do with the tools used, sometimes with the policies and rules, and sometimes with cultural issues.

For tricky cases, we draw a cause-effect diagram to identify the consequences and root causes of this bug and use that to generate concrete proposals for how to avoid this type of bug in the future. Here is an example:

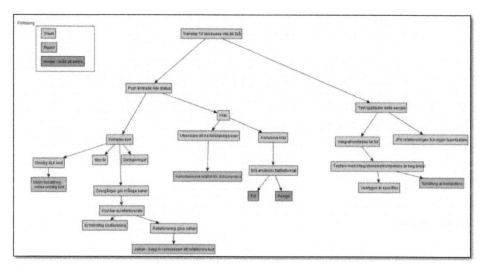

The bug they were analyzing had to do with certain transactions that had gotten lost when communicating with another system. The team came up with four proposals to reduce these types of bugs in the future:

- Remove unnecessary code in one specific module.
- Set up routines to ensure more time for refactoring.
- Focus more on face-to-face communication and less on documentation.
- Work more closely with testers during development to spread competence.

Cause-effect diagrams are a great way to do root-cause analysis, especially when you start finding vicious loops such as the following:

Diana: *Why did we create this bug?*

Phil: *Because we didn't test properly.*

Diana: *Why didn't we test properly?'*

Phil: *Because we were stressed.*

Diana: *Why were we stressed?*

Phil: *Because we were behind on the release plan.*

Diana: *Why were we behind on the release plan?*

Phil: *Because of bugs in the previous release...*

Pretty vicious, huh?

Jerry Weinberg puts it nicely: "Things are the way they are because they *got that way.*"

Or here's another one (don't know who said it first): "If all you ever do is all you've ever done, then all you'll ever get is all you ever got."

Anyway, if you want to learn more about cause-effect diagrams, check out Chapter 20, *Cause-Effect Diagrams*, on page 131.

If you do cause-effect analysis on your bugs, you'll find that bugs aren't really a problem; they are a *symptom*. Bugs in your product are a symptom of bugs in your *process*. If you focus on fixing your process, you'll dramatically reduce the number of new bugs in your product. It's just like if you focus on fire prevention, you'll reduce the need for fire fighting.

So, in the next chapter, I'll show you how we continuously improve our development process.

CHAPTER 10

Continuously Improving the Process

Our process was by no means designed up front. I would never have been able to figure all this out, especially not alone. And even if I could, there would be no buy-in from the project participants, so any process designed up front would never have reached further than the document it was written on.

Our process was *discovered* rather than designed. The first thing I did was put in place a *process improvement engine*. Well, I didn't use those words, but that is in effect what it was. The basic formula is as follows:

- *Clarity*: Have physical boards in prominent locations that show everyone what is going on. And have a clear goal for the delivery that everyone can understand.

- *Communication*: Do process improvement workshops on a regular basis (weekly or biweekly), both locally within each team and at the cross-team level.

- *Data*: Track some simple metrics that show us whether our process is improving. We measure velocity and cycle time (see Chapter 12, *Capturing and Using Process Metrics*, on page 73).

The strategy is pretty simple: it's based on the assumption that people inherently want to succeed with their projects and that people inherently like to solve problems and improve their way of working. So, create an environment that enables and encourages these behaviors.

If everyone knows where we are going and where we are right now and if we have the right communication forums in place, then chances are people will self-organize to move in the right direction and continuously figure out ways of getting there faster.

This mind-set of motivating people to do evolutionary process improvement is the basis of both Agile and Lean.

10.1 Team Retrospectives

Our process improvement workshops are basically Scrum-style sprint retrospectives. By convention, the feature teams use the term *retrospective* for their process improvement workshops, and the cross-team uses the term *process improvement workshop*, so we'll stick to that terminology here.

Each team has a retrospective every week or two, and the length varies from thirty minutes to two hours. Some teams just stand at their taskboard and do the retrospective; some go off to a separate room. Once we even went to a local pub. Usually the team lead facilitates the meeting, but sometimes they pull in someone else (like me).

Bringing in a team-external facilitator from time to time is usually a good idea because that gives the team some variation in how the retrospective is run and provides the team lead with insights about different ways to run retrospectives. And it allows the team lead to participate fully instead of facilitating.

One simple and cheap way to get an external facilitator is for team lead A to facilitate the retrospective of team B, and vice versa.

How the retrospectives are run can vary a great deal, but the goal is the same in every case: reflect on what is working well and what isn't, and decide what to change.

Typical changes include the following:

- Check in code more often.
- Change the time of the daily meeting or how the meeting is run.
- Update the code conventions.
- Identify a new team-internal role such as "build führer" (keeps the build clean) or "goal keeper" (protects the team from disruptions).

Another important function of the team-level retrospectives is to identify escalation points, that is, problems and improvement proposals that affect more than just this team and need to be solved together with the other teams. These are noted by the team leads and brought to the higher-level process improvement workshops.

10.2 Process Improvement Workshops

The process improvement workshop is basically a *scrum of scrums* type of retrospective, with one person from each team and each specialty (the same "cross-team" that meets at the project board at 10 a.m. every day). This is the most effective place to trigger larger changes, such as those that affect multiple teams, and to follow up on the result of previous changes.

The stated purpose of this meeting is to *clarify and improve our way of working*. One of my most important tasks as coach was to set up and facilitate these process improvement workshops until they became part of the culture.

Initially we did these every Thursday at 1 p.m. Having it on Thursdays at 1 p.m. was mostly a coincidence—that was the least congested time for everyone involved. After a month or so, we reduced it to a biweekly meeting, every second Thursday at 1 p.m. The reason we did it so often in the beginning was because of the growth pain and confusion we were experiencing. We needed to quickly improve collaboration between the different specialties, and that meant lots of experimentation.

Having the process improvement workshop every week was rather intense, though; we barely had time to execute the changes from one meeting to the next. The positive side was that the frequent workshops drove us to implement change quickly, because it is embarrassing to sit down at the next process improvement workshop and say, "Well, dang, we never actually got around to implementing that change." Also, because the workshops were held every week, we had to keep them short and focused, which forced us to prioritize only the most important changes and take small steps in our change process.

Come to think of it, the meetings weren't really that short. We started with sixty minutes and had to increase to ninety minutes because we kept running over. That's a pretty long time for a meeting that happens every week. And the changes we made were rather significant, not really baby steps at all. Looking back, I can't say whether that was a good thing or not. We did need to change things quickly (if nothing else, because of the Big Scary Deadline looming around the corner). But the rate of change also caused confusion, especially for the majority of the people who weren't in the cross-team and who saw lots of change happening without always being given a chance to understand or discuss the change.

Once the most important problems were solved, we could slow down the rate of change to a more comfortable level, so we made the workshops biweekly instead. This felt more humane. Now we could spend ninety minutes without feeling as stressed (since it wasn't every week), and it was easier to implement a change and see results before the next meeting.

When doing process improvement workshops, I take care to move away all tables and create a ring of chairs in the center of the room near a whiteboard.

This arrangement has a noticeable effect on the level of collaboration and focus in the room. Everyone is facing each other without any barriers between them and without distractions such as papers and computers on the table.

Each process improvement workshop follows the same basic structure, which roughly corresponds to the meeting structure defined in Diana Larsen and Esther Derby's book *Agile Retrospectives: Making Good Teams Great* [DL06].

At a high level, here's the process:

1. *Set the stage*: Open up the meeting and set the theme and focus.

2. *Gather data*: Go through what has happened since the last meeting, including victories and pain points. If we have a theme, go through concrete data relevant to that theme.

3. *Generate insights*: Discuss the data and what it means to us, focus on the most important pain points, and identify concrete options to alleviate them.

4. *Decide what to do*: Make decisions about which changes to implement.

5. *Close the meeting*: Decide who is going to do what and what will happen by next meeting.

I start by doing a quick round-robin of some sort to get everyone talking—for example, "What is your feeling right now, using one word?" or "What is the most important thing you hope to get out of this meeting?"

I then remind everyone of the purpose of the meeting and mention what the focus of today's meeting is. Sometimes we have a specific focus (such as motivation, metrics, collaboration, test automation, or whatever). Sometimes we have no specific focus other than the general goal of improving our way of working.

Next we summarize key events that have occurred since last meeting and follow up on any decisions and actions from that meeting.

We then quickly summarize what is working well and generally positive developments during the past few weeks. Sometimes I have the participants write sticky notes and put them up on the wall; other times they just talk and I write on the whiteboard. Noticing and celebrating improvement is important to fuel further improvement.

Next we quickly summarize the current pain points and challenges. If there are many (which there usually are), we do some kind of prioritization, typically using dot voting or similar techniques. Dot voting means each person in the room gets three dots to spread out across all the items, based on perceived importance.

Here is an example that shows two columns of sticky notes: "Victories" and "Challenges."

Digression:

> Any Lean enthusiasts of the more fundamentalist type reading this book might point an accusing finger now and say, "Yuck, that's all subjective, touchy-feely stuff! Process improvement must be driven by quantitative, objective data and reports!"
>
> Well, I don't agree. Complex product development of this sort is a creative process done by creative people, and the most important currency is *motivation*. In this context, gut feel beats hard metrics. If something *feels* like an important problem, it most likely is an important problem, whether or not we have metrics to prove it. And the nice thing about gut feel is that it often is a leading indicator of a problem that's *about to occur*, while hard metrics often show a problem only *after* it has occurred.
>
> So yes, we use hard metrics (see Chapter 12, *Capturing and Using Process Metrics*, on page 73), and sometimes those metrics will trigger the necessary gut-feel realization that there is a problem (the proverbial "Oh shit!" moment). But we use metrics primarily to *support* process improvement, not to *drive* it.

Anyway, where were we? Oh yes, so we list the pain points and prioritize them, and we choose one or two of the most important to focus on for this meeting. Then we break out into groups of two or three to discuss and analyze the problem and possible solutions.

Sometimes the solution is fairly simple and obvious. For more complex or recurring problems, we do a root-cause analysis using cause-effect diagrams and similar techniques (see Chapter 20, *Cause-Effect Diagrams*, on page 131), propose some research that will bring useful metrics to the next process improvement workshop, or plan a separate problem-solving workshop to be done with a small focus team.

The breakout discussions usually result in several concrete proposals, or options, which I list on the whiteboard. The default option is always the status quo ("Don't change anything"), a reminder of what will happen if we don't agree on any other option by the end of this meeting.

For each option (including the status quo option), we brainstorm the most obvious advantages and disadvantages. Quite often this quick analysis clearly reveals which option is best, so we agree on implementing that option. For less obvious choices, we do a quick thumb vote to check how people feel about each option.

"I like this option."

 "This option isn't great but acceptable." Or "I don't have a strong opinion and will go with the group." Or "I can't make up my mind right now."

 "This option sucks, and I will not support it."

Sometimes we use "fist of five" instead, which is pretty much the same thing but more granular. Instead of just thumb up, sideways, or down, each person holds up one to five fingers.

 "This is a great option!"

 "This is a pretty good option."

 "This option is not great but acceptable." Or "I don't have a strong opinion and will go with the group." Or "I can't make up my mind right now."

 "I don't like this option and I won't support it. But I may be convinced."

 "Over my dead body!"

The important thing with both of these techniques is that thumb sideways, or three fingers, is the consensus threshold. Any option that has that level of support (or higher) from every person in the workshop is good to go. Everybody doesn't have to *like* that option, but everyone will *accept* and *support* it. That's what consensus means.

This type of consensus voting usually reveals the best option quite clearly. If there are many options and the result is not clear, we start by crossing out any unacceptable options—that is, options that have any votes of one or two fingers or thumb down. Those options don't have group consensus—they are essentially vetoed. Then we look at the remaining options and pick the one that seems to have the strongest support. Again, status quo is the default if we can't agree on any other option.

In the rare case that we have two options with equally strong support, we pick one at random, pick the easiest one, or do a quick tie-breaker vote ("Given a choice between options D and E, which one would you prefer?"). As facilitator of the meeting, I usually decide on the decision process in each case, to avoid getting into time-consuming meta-discussions about how to decide on the decision process (always a risk with smart people). It is up to the meeting participants to protest if they don't like the chosen decision process.

All this consensus-building stuff might sound inefficient, but it is actually quick and effective in most cases. And in the few cases where it isn't quick, that usually means some deeper analysis needs to happen.

Making process improvement decisions means making *changes*. And since we are dealing with people, change means risk of resistance, especially from people who aren't at the meeting where the decision was made. By aiming for 100 percent consensus for each change (that is, 100 percent of the people present at the workshop), we dramatically reduce the risk of resistance and thereby dramatically increase the likelihood that the change will work. So, the few extra minutes spent on consensus building pays off in a big way.

We timebox the meeting strictly, typically to ninety minutes (including a vitally important five-minute break). During the last ten minutes or so we summarize the decisions that we made (list them on the whiteboard) and identify concrete actions—who is going to do what and when.

Here's an example:

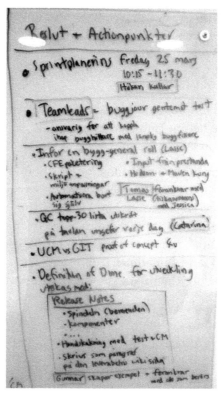

At this meeting we made many decisions (more than usual). The first two were as follows:

- Try the concept of "sprint planning meetings," where the different specialties collaborate to refine and break down user stories and decide which ones to pull into the "Next Ten Features" column on the board. There's more about that in Chapter 13, *Planning the Sprint and Release*, on page 85. If it works well, we'll continue doing sprint planning meetings, probably biweekly (and indeed, it did work out well).

- Each team has a clearly defined "bug contact," the person who testers go to when they find a bug and don't know who should fix it. Team leads are the default bug contact if nobody else is defined.

These changes were easy to make, since they were aimed at solving real-life problems that people were experiencing right now. They were not theoretical solutions to theoretical problems.

Remember that the stated purpose of the meeting is to *clarify and improve our way of working*. Sometimes we don't change anything; instead, we just clarify our current process—that is, resolve some source of confusion and provide a clear description that everyone at the meeting can relay to their teams. One example was when we needed to clarify what we meant by *acceptance test* vs. *system test* vs. *feature test.*

10.3 Managing the Rate of Change

Each weekly process improvement workshop caused a flurry of change, mostly changes for the better. However, after a while, we realized that we were changing too much, too fast.

This was an interesting problem. In most organizations I've worked with, the problem is that there is too *little* process change—everyone is stuck in their current ineffective process. Here we had reached the opposite problem. We were making *lots* of changes, and it takes days or sometimes weeks for a significant process change to ripple through a 60-person project. Many team members got confused (and sometimes frustrated) when the cross-team introduced new changes before the dust from previous changes had settled.

So, we introduced a little bit of bureaucracy to slow down the rate of change. Whenever somebody wants to make a change that affects more than just his own team, they write a *process improvement proposal.* This is a lightweight version of the Lean A3 problem-solving process.[1]

The process improvement proposal template forces you to think about *why* you want to make this change.

- "What problem are you trying to solve?"
- "Who is affected by this change?"
- "What steps are involved in executing this change?"

The answers to these questions are very helpful when determining the value vs. the cost of doing this change. Figure 1, *Example of a Process Improvement Proposal,* on page 63 shows a real-life example of a process improvement proposal (translated to English):

This proposal was about keeping the features at a more customer-valuable level. It also proposed that features estimated to be Large should not be pulled into development at all, since they tend to swell and clog up the process. Instead, they should be broken into smaller deliverables. And when that is done, if the smaller features aren't each independently valuable to the customer, then a title should be written at the top of the card in bold blue text, showing that several smaller features fit together into a bigger feature. This helps keep these features together from a release perspective.

---

1. See www.crisp.se/lean/a3-template.

Proposal: More Customer-Valued Stories

Why? What Problem Are We Trying to Solve?

- Hard to get an overview of the project board from customer perspective, many stories are so small that they can't be delivered.

Who Is Affected By The Change?

- Requirements, development, and test teams.

What Are the Change Implementation Steps?

- Update Definition of Done for "Ready for Development", add "the story is valuable to the customer".
- Go through the board & identify stories that are too small to be valuable. Combine these into bigger stories (as long as they don't exceed Medium).

Example:

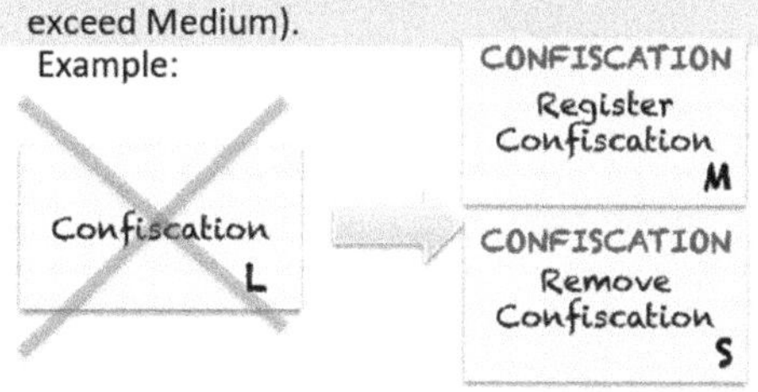
Confiscation
L
CONFISCATION
Register Confiscation
M
CONFISCATION
Remove Confiscation
S

Description / FAQ

A story that goes into development must:

1. Be size S or M
2. Be as customer valuable as possible, as long as we don't break the size rule.

The requirements team ensures that each card under "Ready for Development" is a customer-valued story (regardless of size). However, before it enters development it must be S or M.

Question: What happens if the story is L, and must be delivered as a whole before it is valuable to the customer?

- Break it down to smaller stories (new cards) which are size M, but with highest possible customer value per story.
- Visually group these stories by writing the name of the higher level feature in big blue letters at the top of each card.

Figure 1—Example of a Process Improvement Proposal

Proposals can come from anyone. Typically the person who wrote the proposal shows up at the process improvement workshop to present the proposal and answer questions. Our template essentially turns the proposal into a small business case for a specific change, making it easier to prioritize and make decisions.

The purpose of introducing this little template was to allow us to *limit the amount of change*. So if we get four proposals, we might implement only one or two of them, even if all four of the proposals were great. It is very difficult *not* to implement a great process improvement proposal, but we realized that we have to limit the amount of simultaneous process improvement initiatives. If we don't, we get too much confusion, which offsets the benefit of the process improvement.

We've even considering having a separate *process improvement board* with WIP limits, showing which changes are currently being implemented. That could be useful for follow-up purposes too. But it would be yet another board to find space for and keep up-to-date. Hmmmm…

As you see, Kanban doesn't provide many specific rules. It is up to you to decide things like how many boards to use on a project. That's the beauty (and pain) of Kanban—it's flexible, and you figure things out as you go along. Just stick to this rule of thumb: "When in doubt, choose the simplest solution."

CHAPTER 11

Managing Work in Progress

In any kind of workflow it is useful to distinguish *work states* and *wait states*. When the mail carrier is carrying an envelope to your mailbox, that envelope is in a *work state* (because something is happening to it). When it is in your mailbox, the envelope is in a *wait state* (because nothing is happening to it).

The reason we need mailboxes is because you aren't always there to receive an envelope when the mail carrier arrives. Your mailbox is a *buffer*—a place for things to hang around in while waiting for the next step in the process.

Now if you study the project board closely, you'll see that only four of the columns represent work in progress (WIP). The other six columns are *buffers* (or *queues*), highlighted here:

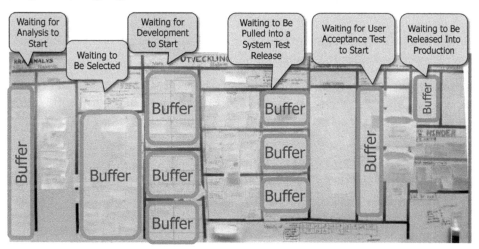

We highlight buffer columns by writing "Queue" in red next to the column title.

It is very useful to distinguish buffer columns from WIP columns, since buffers are clearly waste—the features in there are just sitting there waiting, right? The larger the buffer, the *longer things take*!

Think of your mailbox again. The longer you let stuff accumulate in there, the longer it takes for you to get around to reading any given letter. This translates into waste. You'll need a bigger mailbox, your friends will be frustrated because it takes forever to get a response from you, and your bills won't get paid on time.

Yet, sometimes we need a small buffer to ensure smooth flow between two processes. For example, the rate at which features get developed doesn't always perfectly match the rate at which features get system-tested. This type of buffering can be seen as a "necessary waste."

Imagine a factory, where work items (such as envelopes) flow from left to right:

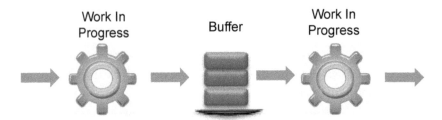

Unless the two machines happen to crank things out at exactly the same rate, we need a buffer to absorb the variability.

As the process improves, however, the need for these buffers is reduced. By clearly visualizing buffers on the board, we are more likely to keep asking ourselves whether we really *need* all these buffers and what we can do to reduce them.

Here is an example of an older version of the board, when we had yet another buffer column called "Wait for Team to Start," between requirements and development. It is marked with an *X* here:

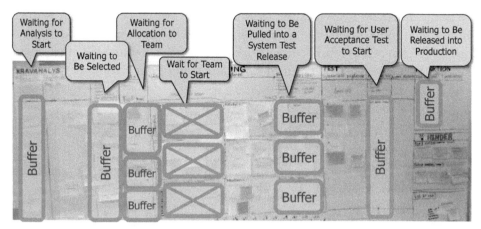

We had that buffer because the teams previously had a more Scrum-like model with *sprints* (the Scrum word for an iteration). For every new sprint, each team would do a sprint planning meeting and commit to a specific set of features. Those were pulled into "Wait for Team to Start." So, we had three buffers between analysis and development:

- Features that have been identified through analysis but have not yet been selected into the "Next Ten Features" list

- Features that are included in the "Next Ten Features" list but have not yet been pulled in by a team

- Features that are in the current sprint of team X but have not yet been started

Here's a factory representation of these three buffers:

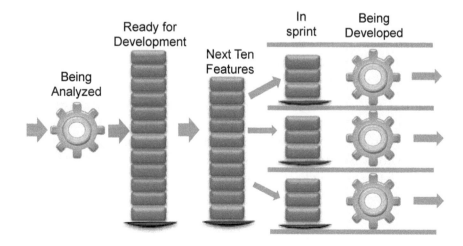

We noticed that we were wasting too much time arguing over which feature should be in which buffer. So, we simply removed the third queue and decided that each team pulls features directly from the top-ten list instead of batching features into sprints. This reduced turbulence and improved flow.

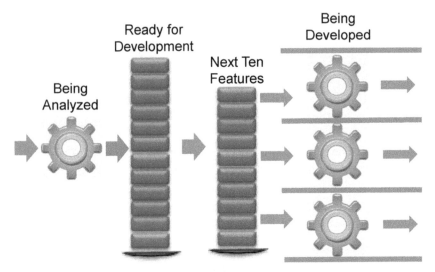

This raises the question of specialization. If a team is working within a specific feature area—for example, integration with system X—then it is most effective for that team to implement all features that integrate with system X, since they have knowledge of how system X works.

That doesn't mean, however, that the team needs to pull in all X-related features up front. Although this team may be the *default choice* for X-related features, we don't want to rule out the possibility of other teams helping out if this team becomes a bottleneck.

So although each team pulls directly from the Next 10 list, they do it in an intelligent way; the teams talk to each during the dev sync meeting and figure out how to best use the current capacity of each team.

To aid in this process, we have *team magnets* on the project board. A team can *tag* a feature in the Next 10 list (or earlier in the workflow) with their team magnet, indicating that "This feature would be best done by our team." That way, people know who to talk to about that feature, and the other teams will think twice before pulling in that feature.

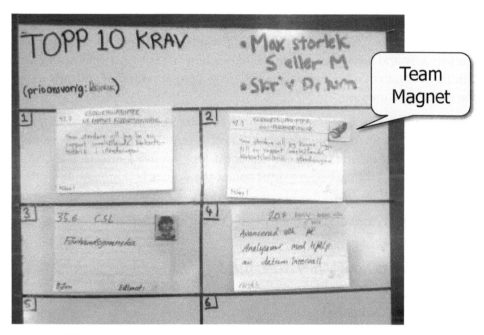

11.1 Using WIP Limits

At the top of each column on the board there is a red number. These are *work in progress limits* (WIP limits), for example "Max Five Features per Team."

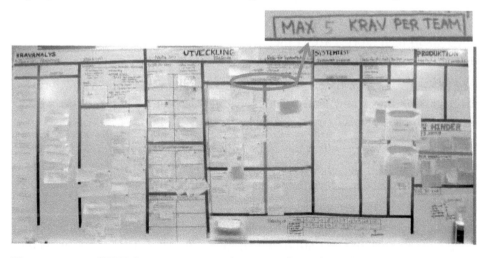

The purpose of WIP limits is to avoid too much multitasking and overloading a downstream process. If the testers have too much work to do, we don't want developers to keep building new features and adding to their work-load—instead, they should focus on helping test. WIP limits act as an alert signal to highlight the problem before it gets out of hand.

This can be likened to a printer. The WIP limit of a typical printer is *one page at a time.* If that paper gets jammed, you want the printer to stop printing immediately and alert you, right? No matter how urgent your printout is, you *don't* try to cram in more pages when there is a paper jam; that will only make the problem worse.

We have WIP limits pretty much across the whole board, written in red text at the top of each column or set of columns. The WIP limit of "Max Five Features per Team" means that if a team is working on five features, they won't start working on a new feature until one of the others is done and in system test.

See *One Day in Kanban Land,* on page 113 for a cartoon illustration of this type of behavior.

11.2 Why WIP Limits Apply Only to Features

Our WIP limits apply only to feature cards. Tech stories and bug fixes aren't included in the WIP limit.

The reason bugs aren't included in the WIP limit (yet) is because they often are quite urgent and quite small. Besides, we don't yet have a very consistent way of handling bugs on the board. Sometimes bugs are on the board, and sometimes they're not, so we don't want to create too many rules around this just yet.

The reason tech stories aren't included in the WIP limit is because, well, let me try to explain....

One of the reasons for having WIP limits is to avoid overloading a downstream process. Building a new feature will certainly add work to test, so if we build features too fast, we will overload test.

Tech stories, however, often have the opposite effect: they *offload* the downstream bottleneck. Many of our tech stories are related to test automation and infrastructure improvements, both of which improve quality and make life easier for testers.

When system test becomes a bottleneck, the test team will focus on finishing their current system test round, which means it will take a few days before they can pull the next batch of cards from "Ready for System Test" to "System Test Ongoing." The WIP limit of five for each development team applies across both columns, "Development in Progress" and "Ready for System Test." The consequence of this is that when system test becomes a bottleneck, the WIP of the development teams will fill up, since the features that they have developed are still stuck on their tray until the system test team pulls them in.

So, what should the developers *do* when their WIP limit is full?

They should do anything that will assist or offload system test! In fact, at one point when system test was badly bottlenecked, one of the testers posted this as "question of the week" on the board to remind people to ask this question every day at the project sync meeting. Very effective!

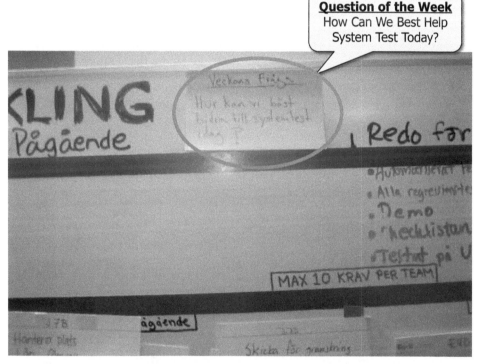

One way to help test is for more people to do manual testing and bug fixing. Another way is to develop more automated tests and improve the test infrastructure. Those things are represented as tech stories. That's why we don't include tech stories in the WIP limit, because we want to *encourage* team members to work on tech stories when the WIP limit is full.

During some periods the teams focused almost entirely on test automation, with only green-dotted cards on the project board. This is a great example of how Kanban boards with WIP limits facilitate self-organization and bottleneck alleviation.

Another reason WIP limits apply only to features is because that's consistent with how we use metrics. When measuring cycle time and calculating velocity, we include only feature cards (for more on that, see Chapter 12, *Capturing and Using Process Metrics*, on page 73). Basically, tech stories and bugs are currently "under the radar" in terms of WIP limits and metrics. That may, of course, change....

As for the "question of the week," that concept turned out to be very useful. Later we made the question more generic (since system test isn't always the bottleneck) and turned it into a prioritized what-do-I-do-today guide:

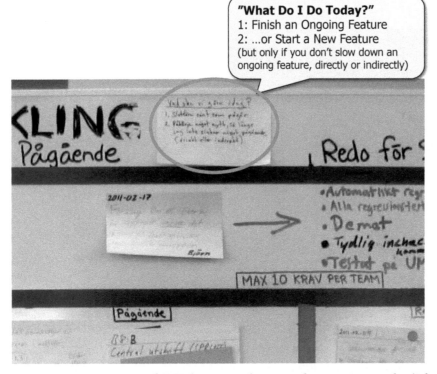

One of the consequences of WIP limits is that people sometimes don't have anything to do. Or more specifically, WIP limits sometimes constrain people to do something different from what they would normally do (for example, help test instead of developing a new feature). In that situation, the prioritized what-do-I-do-today guide on the board is useful.

In fact, this little note captures the essence of WIP limits: focus on finishing things rather than starting things!

So, how do we actually keep track of how good we are at finishing things? That's the topic of the next chapter.

CHAPTER 12

Capturing and Using Process Metrics

Process metrics are useful to find out what needs to be improved and if our changes are doing any good. They can also be useful for high-level release planning.

We track two process metrics:

- Velocity (features per week)
- Cycle time (weeks per feature)

We capture these metrics entirely manually. It's so easy that I'm surprised not all projects do this.

12.1 Velocity (Features per Week)

For velocity (throughput), we just count, at the end of each week, how many features have reached "Ready for Acceptance Test (This Week)." We write this number down in a velocity log at the bottom of the board and then move those cards down to "Ready for Acceptance Test (Past Weeks)" to show that they have already been counted.

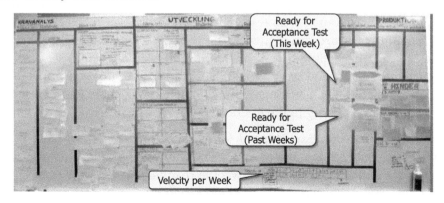

Here is a close-up of the velocity log at the bottom of the board:

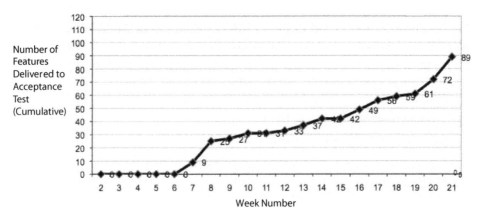

Using this information, we generate a simple burn-up chart, showing the cumulative number of features that have been completed per week.

This information is useful in many ways. First, it's used as a *reality check* tool to make sure that the release plan is realistic, and second, it's used as a tool to predict approximately how many features will be done by a certain date (see Chapter 6, *Tracking the High-Level Goal*, on page 31).

The burn-up chart is also used to highlight problems. For example, during the first few weeks of measurements, the velocity was 0. The teams were working very hard, but system test had become a bottleneck for various reasons, so all the features were queuing up in front of the test team. Everyone could see the cards piling up on the board, and everyone could see that the velocity was 0 week after week. This created a sense of urgency and caused developers to gradually focus more on helping test instead of just developing new features and adding to the queue.

Finally, the burn-up chart is used to visualize process improvement. For example, we could see that our average velocity (the slope of the curve) doubled between Q1 and Q2. These types of visible results help motivate everyone to keep improving the process.

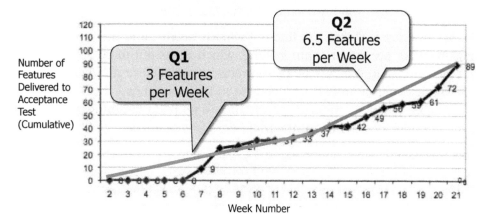

Note, though, that statistics like this need to be used with care. During the weeks after creating this diagram, the curve flattened, since the team focused on internal improvements and had a 0 velocity. A more realistic estimate is that velocity increased by roughly 50 percent rather than doubled.

We've considered measuring the velocity of tech stories as well so we can visualize how effort is distributed between customer needs and tech stories. Combing these two velocities would give us our total capacity, which would give us a smoother burn-up curve and make planning easier.

12.2 Why We Don't Use Story Points

At this point you might be wondering how we can get away with just *counting* the features. What about size? Shouldn't we take size into account when measuring velocity? If velocity doubled between Q1 and Q2, does that really mean we became more productive? Or did we get more features done in Q2 only because those features were smaller?

Isn't this type of simplistic velocity misleading?

In theory, yes. In practice, however, the feature sizes turned out to be quite evenly distributed. I did a little experiment and assigned each feature a *weight* based on estimated size, so Small = 1kg, Medium = 2kg, and Large = 3kg. Most agile teams would call this a *story point*—that is, a relative estimate of the effort involved in building that feature.

Here's a useful metaphor. Suppose I'm loading bricks, and suppose I want to measure velocity for this. My velocity turns out to be ten to fifteen bricks per minute. That's not a very exact number. But wait, the bricks have different weights! What if we measure kg per minute, instead of bricks per minute?

That might give us a smoother velocity and therefore make it easier to predict how many bricks I will have loaded by the end of the day.

So, we measure each brick to find out what it weighs, and then we calculate how many kg per minute I am loading, which turns out to be 20–30 kg per minute. Um, wait, this was no more precise than the first number, which is 10–15 bricks per minute! X ± 50 percent in both cases! As long as the bricks are roughly evenly distributed in size, there's no point weighing each one to calculate velocity. Just count the number of bricks instead.

This was exactly what happened in our case. I created a burn-up chart with kg instead of number of features, and the shape was just as jagged as before. The higher level of precision gave no added value, so estimating in story points would have been a waste of time.

12.3 Cycle Time (Weeks per Feature)

The other thing we measure is *cycle time* (or flow time). Cycle time means how long it takes for something to get done, or, more specifically in our case, "How long did it take for feature X to move from "Next Ten Features" to "Ready for Acceptance Test.""

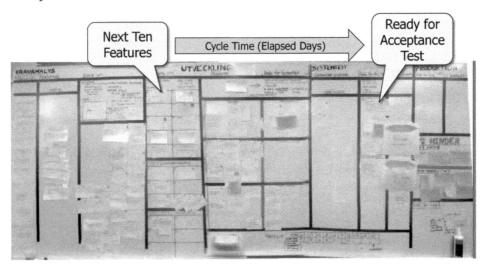

Cycle time is also very easy to measure. Every time a feature is selected to be among the "Next Ten Features," we write a start date on the card.

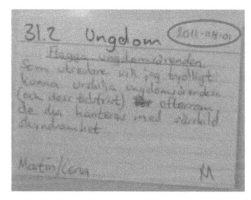

Every time a feature reaches "Ready for Acceptance Test," we note the finish date and write down the elapsed days for that feature in a spreadsheet.

Leverabel	start	slut	Genomströmningstid (dagar)
6A	2011-02-01	2011-02-17	16
6A	2011-02-01	2011-02-17	16
26B	2011-02-03	2011-02-24	21
26A	2011-02-03	2011-02-24	21
B2.2	2011-02-08	2011-02-21	13
25.2.1	2011-02-08	2011-02-18	10
25.2.2	2011-02-08	2011-03-25	45
B8-A	2011-02-10	2011-03-09	27
T23.2	2011-02-10	2011-02-23	13
16J	2011-02-20	2011-03-28	36
A-4A	2011-03-08	2011-03-30	22

We then visualize this using a control chart, where the height of each bar represents how long one specific feature took to cross the board.

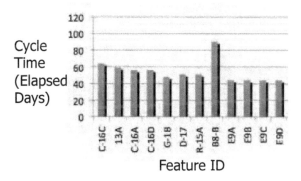

This graph is useful for predicting how long it will take for a feature to get done. It's also a great way to generate a sense of horrified awe, because most people don't realize how long things really take! It happens almost every time a company starts visualizing this stuff.

\\// **Joe asks:**

〜 # Why Don't You Measure Cycle Time All the Way to Production?

Because of Powers Beyond Our Control, we release roughly every second month. These dates are fairly fixed, and the last week or two before each release is an acceptance test phase where real users come in to try the system. Thus, whenever a feature reaches "Ready for Acceptance Test," it will be stuck there until the end of the release cycle. These are the remains from our waterfall history....

We measure cycle time only up to "Ready for Acceptance Test" because that's the part of the workflow we can control (and hence optimize). Also, our experience was that serious problems were rarely found in acceptance test. So, by measuring cycle time up to "Ready for Acceptance Test," we cover the riskiest part of the workflow, which is good enough for us.

Quite typically, the elapsed time is five to ten times longer than the actual worked time. So, it might take twenty days of calendar time to finish a feature that is actually only three days of work. This discrepancy is usually caused by things such as multitasking or the abundance of buffers and queues for features to get stuck in while waiting for the next step in the process.

The good news is that once you understand your cycle time, it's usually not too hard to shorten it dramatically, using techniques such as limiting WIP (see Chapter 11, *Managing Work in Progress*, on page 65). The following trend line shows how our cycle time was cut in half within a few months:

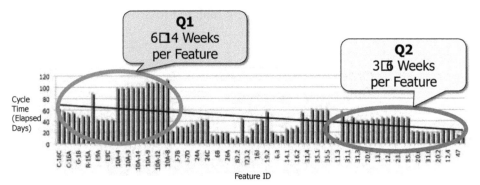

Another interesting thing that we noticed was the lack of correlation between feature size and cycle time. In the next diagram, the features are color-coded based on their original estimate:

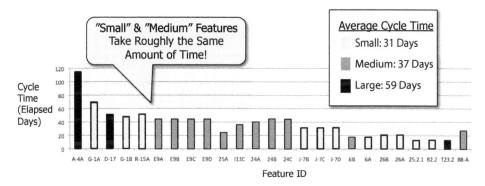

As you can see, some of the *small* features took as long as seven weeks, while some *large* features took as little as two weeks. It turned out that size wasn't the main factor influencing cycle time; other factors such as focus and access to key people were more important.

At one point we went through this data and, to guide the improvement efforts, set challenging but realistic targets:

- *More stable velocity*: Velocity should be roughly the same every week instead of unevenly distributed. This would give us fewer bottlenecks, easier release planning, and smoother flow in general.

- *Higher velocity*: Our average was three; we set the target to five.

- *Lower cycle time*: Our average was six weeks (but shrinking fast); we set the target to two.

As we defined these targets, an interesting insight dawned on us. Suppose we reach the first two targets and get to a stable velocity of five features per week. What would that mean for the third target of decreasing cycle time?

Our data (and photos) shows that, on any given day, typically thirty or so features were on the project board in various buffers and WIP states.

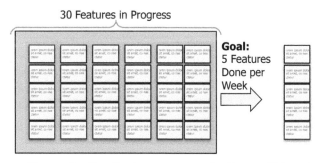

That means, mathematically, that average cycle time will be six weeks!

Suppose you are at a pizza restaurant and their delivery capacity is five pizzas per hour. How long will you have to wait for your pizza?

Twelve minutes?

No, not if there are thirty other people in the restaurant, all waiting for their pizza. In that case, the average wait time would be six hours!

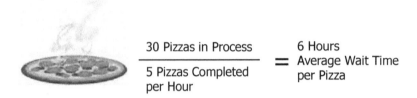

The same math applies to our feature development.

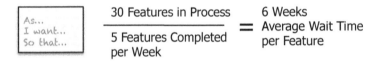

This by the way is known as Little's law[1] in queuing theory. It is inescapable.

So, how do we improve cycle from six weeks to two weeks? Well, either increase velocity by a factor of 3 (which would cost time and effort!) or reduce WIP by a factor 3. Which do you think is cheaper? Exactly!

So, the teams reduced their WIP limit from ten to five features per team:

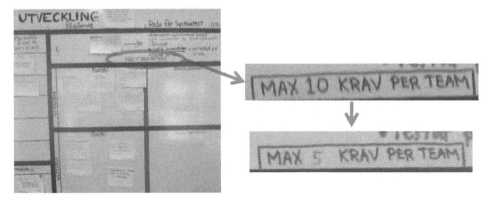

---

1. http://en.wikipedia.org/wiki/Little's_law

OK, that reduction isn't by a factor of 3, but it's still a significant reduction. When reducing WIP, you need to take into account that, if you reduce it too much, you'll see other side effects such as having lots of people with nothing to do. That in turn negatively impacts velocity and thereby increases cycle time again. So, you have to find a balance.

The goal is to have a low enough WIP limit to keep people collaborating and to expose problems—but not low enough to expose all problems at once (which just causes frustration and unstable flow).

We haven't reached the target of two weeks per feature yet, but that's not terribly important. The purpose of the target is to keep us moving in the right direction. We've cut cycle time in half, and the act of reducing WIP was one of the many things that helped us achieve this.

And it's nice to have metrics to show us we're moving in the right direction.

12.4 Cumulative Flow

The Kanban board shows us bottlenecks in real time, which is great, but it does not show us historical trends.

Cumulative flow diagrams are a popular tool in Kanban circles to visualize bottlenecks over time. Every day, count how many items are in each column. Then visualize it in a diagram like this:

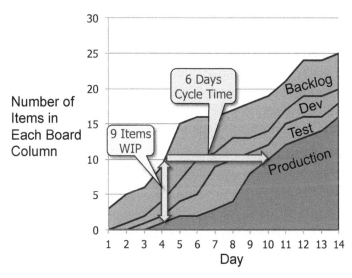

Each color represents one column on the board, and each tick on the x-axis represents one day. The vertical stack shows how many items were in which column on that day. Theoretically this will illustrate how bottlenecks move over time, where there are obstructions to flow, and how increased WIP correlates to longer cycle time.

Great tool. In theory.

"In theory, theory and practice are the same. In practice, they are not."

—Yogi Berra

In practice, this hasn't worked for us so far. Here's our cumulative flow diagram:

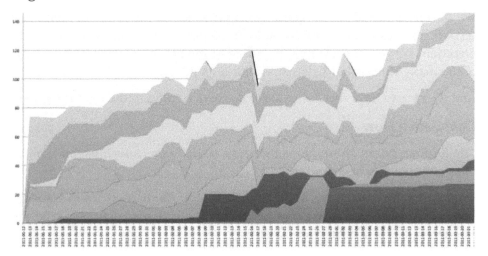

It's hard to draw any useful conclusions from this. And any conclusions we might draw are likely to be wrong. For example, in the middle of the timeline it looks like we suddenly removed a bunch of work, but what actually happened is that we decided to stop including tech stories in the count. In some situations we *parked* some features on the side of the board because they were essentially paused, and the person counting the stories on the board every day didn't include them. These stories then reappeared later.

Our cumulative flow diagram turned out to be very *brittle* in the sense that it would become inaccurate and misleading whenever we made changes to the structure of the board or deviated from the standard flow.

We are still dutifully collecting this data, though, mostly because I keep hearing from other coaches and Lean folks that cumulative flow diagrams are useful. It takes only a few minutes per day for one person, so who knows? Maybe it will become useful some day....

12.5 Process Cycle Efficiency

We don't measure process cycle efficiency, but I mention it here because it's one of those things we kind of wish we did measure. If our Kanban board was mirrored in an electronic system, we would definitely measure process cycle efficiency, but in our currently pure manual Kanban system, it would be too fiddly.

Anyway, here's what it means:

$$\text{Process Cycle Efficiency (\%)} = \frac{\text{Touch Time}}{\text{Elapsed Time}}$$

Elapsed time means how many days the feature took to cross the project board (= cycle time).

Touch time means how many days the feature was actually worked on (or "touched"). In other words, it's how many days that card spent in *work in progress* columns, as opposed to queue/buffer columns.

This gives us very interesting data such as "Hey, feature X was only two days of work but took twenty days to cross the board! That's only 10 percent process cycle efficiency!"

Most companies are in the 10–15 percent range unless they specifically optimize for this. Trying to drive this number up is a great way to uncover and eliminate waste.

CHAPTER 13

Planning the Sprint and Release

The purpose of sprint planning meetings is to figure out what to do next. In our case, that means deciding which features go into the "Next Ten Features" column.

Our meetings aren't really Scrum-by-the-book sprint planning meetings. In Scrum, the team is supposed to commit to a specific set of features for the next sprint. We don't do that. We don't even have sprints. All we want is to agree on which features are next in line. Our velocity isn't stable enough to be able to predict how many features will get done in the short term.

The meeting has two parts: backlog grooming and top ten selection.

13.1 Backlog Grooming

Backlog grooming is all about getting features to the "Ready for Development" state (see Chapter 7, *Defining Ready and Done*, on page 35).

We do this during the first half of the sprint planning meeting. The requirements team presents the next features to be developed (yes, the requirements team fulfills the equivalent of the product owner role in Scrum, mostly because they are closest to the customer and users).

Then we break the group into small cross-functional subgroups, typically with one requirements analyst, one developer, and one tester in each. Each subgroup takes a few feature cards, estimates them using Planning Poker (see Chapter 19, *Sizing the Backlog with Planning Poker*, on page 125), and writes S, M, or L on the card (representing Small/Medium/Large). If the card is Large, they break it down further or decide to leave it out of "Next Ten Features" for the time being (we don't allow Large features into development). They also discuss and agree on a suitable acceptance test and write it on the backside.

13.2 Selecting the Top Ten Features

Now we look at the pile of features at hand and discuss which ones should go into the "Next Ten Features" column on the project board (and, more importantly, which ones *shouldn't*). Usually the "Next Ten Features" list isn't empty to begin with—there may be two to three or so features already there. In that case, we evaluate those features against the new ones. The theme of the conversation is "Out of everything in the whole world that we might focus on next, what are the top ten features?"

Several aspects influence this decision:

- *Business value*—which features will the customers be happiest to see?
- *Knowledge*—which features will generate knowledge (and thereby reduce risk)?
- *Resource utilization*—we want a balance of feature areas so that each team has stuff to work on.
- *Dependencies*—which features are best built together?
- *Testability*—which features are most logical to test together and should therefore be developed in close proximity to each other?

13.3 Why We Moved Backlog Grooming Out of the Sprint Planning Meeting

After doing a few sprint planning meetings, we noticed that backlog grooming took quite long, and sometimes the sprint planning meeting felt hurried as a result. We wanted to keep the meeting timeboxed and focused.

So, recently we've started doing backlog grooming separately, *before* the sprint planning meeting. Typically, a few days before the sprint planning meeting, one of the requirements analysts will have an informal conversation with a developer and a tester to discuss an upcoming feature. As a result of the conversation, that feature would be broken down, estimated, and given an acceptance test.

We still do some grooming during the sprint planning meeting, but we prefer to do as much grooming as possible before the sprint planning meeting. I see this trend in many other organizations, as well.

13.4 Planning the Release

We know our velocity: it used to be three features per week on average, and now it's four to five. This information is useful for long-term release planning. We don't know exactly what our velocity will be in the future, but it is probably safe to assume that it will be in the range of three to five features per week, on average.

So, if someone wants to know "How long will it will take implement this?" (waving a list of feature areas) or "How much of this can we get done by Christmas?" we can give a realistic answer—as long as we know the number of features.

The problem is, for long-term planning we don't know the number of features. All we have is a bunch of vague ideas. We might call these *epics* or *feature areas*. Some can be really, really huge!

As mentioned in Section 12.2, *Why We Don't Use Story Points*, on page 75, we don't estimate features in story points because it turned out that sizes were fairly evenly distributed, so story points wouldn't add value. However, for *long-term planning* that logic doesn't hold, since we are looking mostly at *epics* rather than specific features. Although our velocity of three to five features per week may include an occasional epic, it would be unrealistic to expect us to complete three to five epics per week!

The solution is simple. Take each epic and estimate how many features it will break into. This estimation (like all other estimation) requires effort from requirements analysts, developers, and testers. The process is similar to estimating in story points; we are just asking "How many features is this epic?" instead of "How many story points?"

Once we have estimated the number of features for each epic, we can count the total number of features and divide by our historic velocity of three to five features per week. This gives us just enough information to be able to say something like, "We can probably build all of this in six to twelve months." It's still only a rough estimate, but it's based on real data.

As velocity stabilizes, we can make better and better predictions, so our answer might become more precise: eight to ten months (as long as we don't change the team size too much).

This way of planning is not quite part of the culture yet; we still have a tendency to fall back to the more traditional "estimate the hours of effort per feature and then add it all up," which takes a long time to calculate and often results in an unrealistic plan (because it isn't based on empirical data such as velocity). But we're getting there.

One thing we learned the hard way is that release planning in a multiteam project is almost impossible without a well-oiled version control system. On to the next chapter.

CHAPTER 14

How We Do Version Control

Because we've been doing pretty rapid development of a complex system in a multiteam scenario, we've had plenty of challenges to deal with. One lesson we've learned is that we should have gotten our version control system in shape before we scaled from thirty to sixty people. For long periods our version control system had seriously broken trunks and branches. In fact, at one point the teams even set up a dedicated Kanban board for all the problems in the trunk!

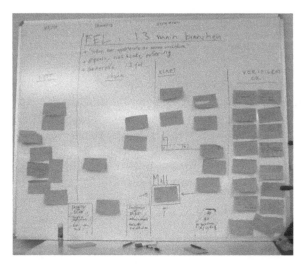

To avoid this problem in the future, we decided to implement the *mainline model*, a stable-trunk pattern described in my article "Agile Version Control with Multiple Teams."[1] That change was a bumpy ride, but it certainly helped us get things into order!

Here's what we did.

---

1.   http://www.infoq.com/articles/agile-version-control

14.1 No Junk on the Trunk

For a project of this size, it's critically important to have a stable trunk at all times. Stable in our case means ready for system test. This maps directly to the project board column with the same name and the *definition of ready for system test* that's written above it (see Section 7.2, *Ready for System Test*, on page 37).

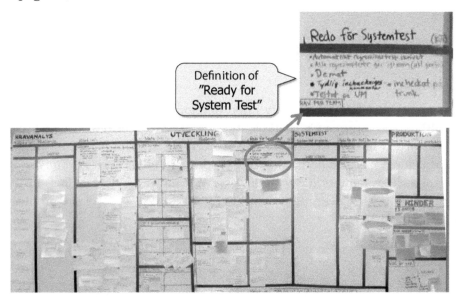

When a feature has been developed, we thoroughly test it at the feature level *before* checking it in to the trunk and *before* moving the card to the "Ready for System Test" column. Once it passes these tests, we check the code in to the trunk and move the card.

This means that, from the trunk's perspective, the product grows in discrete steps, while always remaining stable and ready for system test.

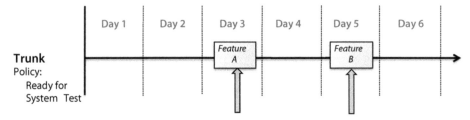

Now, since we're all human, we sometimes make mistakes and check in things that break the trunk. That's OK, as long as the mistakes are discovered quickly and fixed (or rolled back). Our continuous integration system continuously monitors the trunk and runs builds and tests whenever something is checked in. If something is wrong, a lava lamp turns an angry color and alerts us. The continuous integration system can't verify everything, but it will catch the most obvious issues such as broken builds or failing unit tests.

14.2 Team Branches

Each team has a *team branch* that they use to check in and share code during development (some teams have several different types of team branches). Team branches have more lenient policies than the trunk. The code has to compile, and all unit tests have to pass, but the feature doesn't have to be finished or tested. The team branch is there to provide a place for developers to check in unfinished code.

So, how do we keep the trunk and the team branches and all individual workstations in sync? Here's a summary of how change flows through the system:

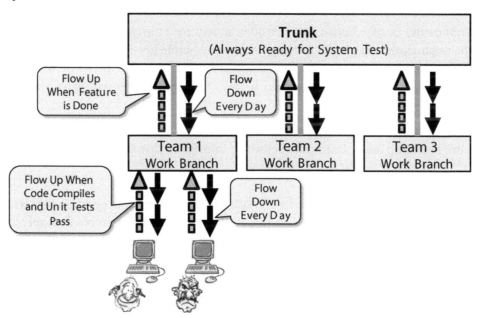

Basically, change flows "downward" (from the trunk to the team branches to the workstations) on a continuous basis and flows "upward" (from workstations to team branches to the trunk) at stable points.

Every morning the team leads merge down any changes from the trunk to their team branch, handling any merge conflicts immediately. Similarly, each developer will merge down any changes from their team branch to their workstation on a fairly continuous basis.

Whenever a developer feels that his code is stable enough to share with other team members (that is, the code compiles and the unit tests pass), he will check in the code on the team branch.

Whenever the team feels that they have completed a feature and tested it as well as they can, they will do the following:

- Merge down from the trunk to the team branch (in case the trunk has been updated by other teams today).

- Do a final check to ensure that the team branch is stable (that is, ready for system test).

- Merge the team branch up into the trunk.

At that moment in time, the team branch and trunk contain exactly the same code! This brief moment of glory lasts until a developer checks in something new on the team branch.

This model is nice because it provides a way for changes to ripple through the organization in a rapid but consistent way, while keeping the trunk stable. Anything that appears on the trunk will usually be on all team branches and all developer workstations within a day, and any merge conflicts will be resolved quickly.

Unmerged branches (or diverging code) are a form of technical debt, and we were suffering badly from that before we moved to this stable trunk model.

14.3 System Test Branch

System test goes on more or less continuously (rather than just at the end of the release cycle). Since system test is all about how the features fit together as whole, we need a stable version of the system to run the tests on. That is, with the exception of bug fixes, we don't want features being added and updated while system test is going on.

We manage this using *system test branches*. Whenever we are ready for a new round of system tests, we spawn off a system test branch from the trunk. Since the trunk is always ready for system test (except when we've goofed), the test team can do that immediately. The dirty stuff is in the team branches, so there's no need to wait.

Once we've created the system test branch, we deploy that version to a system test environment and start running system tests. The automated regression tests were run before merging the features to the trunk, so during system test we do mostly manual scenario testing and exploratory testing to catch the more subtle bugs. This version of the system is isolated from any change happening on the trunk, giving the testers a nice stable release to test on.

If we find a bug in system test, a developer fixes that bug directly on the system test branch and directly merges the fix down to the trunk. That way, bug fixes reach all teams quickly, and we can be sure the fix will be included in future releases.

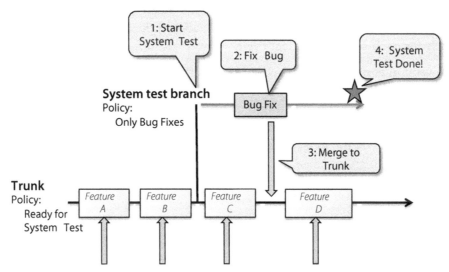

System testing is complete when no system-level problems can be found on that version. There may be key features missing, so we might not be ready for acceptance test yet, but the features implemented so far seem to work together. Great!

What do we do now? Well, we start over again! System test takes days and sometimes weeks. During this time new teams are adding functionality to the trunk. So, we create a new system test branch from the latest version on the trunk, deploy that to the system test environment, and run a new series of system tests. And so on.

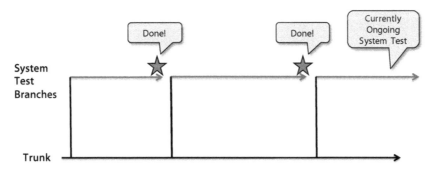

This way of working ensures that we always have a stable version that we could release to acceptance test. When problems are found in system test, we can solve them fairly quickly, since only a limited amount of code has changed since last system test. Over time, each system test cycle gradually becomes shorter.

We don't always run *all* system tests. Sometimes we choose a suitable subset, depending on which parts of the system have been modified and how close we are to the release date. This is a risk trade-off decision that's done separately for each new system test cycle.

The version control system is really the heart of any multiteam development project. As the organization becomes more Lean and Agile, the version control system usually needs to be evolved as well. So, keep an eye on this. Find out how long it takes to change one single line of code and get it into production. That may well be the most important metric in the project!

CHAPTER 15

Why We Use Only Physical Kanban Boards

So, why do we use this big, messy, icky, analog thing with tape and sticky notes and handwritten text when we have plenty of slick electronic tools to choose from? Most of those electronic tools can automagically generate all kinds of detailed statistics, be backed up, be accessed from outside the building, have different views, and so on. Why don't we use something like that instead?

One of the main reasons is *evolution*.

Our board has changed structure many times. It took a couple of months before it started stabilizing. Only then did we start using black tape to mark the columns—before that we used hand-drawn lines because they changed so often. But we can still move the tape if we need to do so.

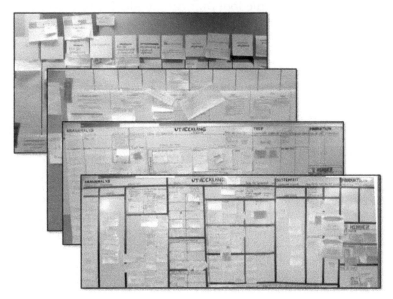

Here are some examples of changes that have happened:

- Adding or removing columns
- Adding or removing swim lanes, sometimes within a column, sometimes across the whole board
- Adding a new type of item on the board (index card, sticky note, magnet, colored tape)
- Writing down policy statements such as "definition of done"
- Writing down metrics such as velocity
- Adding color dimensions such as "red text means defect" or "pink sticky means impediment"
- Using envelopes to group all features that were released together, and writing the release version number on the cover
- Allowing some items to be placed on the border between two teams because they are being shared between them
- Dividing one feature into many subfeatures, and keeping them together by writing a keyword at the top of each subfeature

Each of these changes is trivial to implement. Anybody, even a five-year-old, could implement any of these changes physically on the board once we know exactly what we want it to look like.

I have yet to see any electronic tool that can do all of this—except possibly a generic drawing program like Google Drawing. And if we add the rule that anybody should be able to implement the change within fifteen minutes without any training—well, in that case a physical card wall is hard to beat.

At one point we redesigned the whole board based on this sketch:

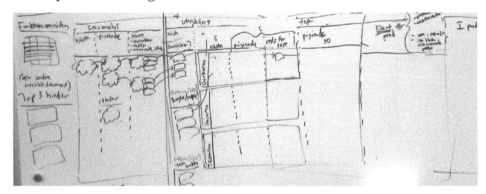

It took about one hour to create the actual board based on this sketch. Once again, most electronic tools I've seen can't do this. And the ones that can require expert-level knowledge.

The second reason we use a physical board: *collaboration.*

The "daily cocktail party" I described in Chapter 3, *Attending the Daily Cocktail Party*, on page 13 would be very difficult to do without physical boards.

If we had an electronic Kanban board, we could use a projector to display it on the wall. But we would lose most of the interaction, the part where people pick up a card from the wall and wave it while talking about it, or where people write stuff on the cards or move them around during the meeting. People would most likely update the board while sitting at their desk—which is more convenient but less collaborative.

One clear pattern I've noticed with all my clients is that boards like this can change the culture of an organization, and this definitely happened in the PUST project. I could see how the patterns of interaction changed and how trust between the teams improved by collaborating in front of the board every day. During our first project-level retrospective, one of the first items that came up under *keep doing* was "keep using Kanban boards to visualize the work."

We do have several electronic tracking systems to complement the physical Kanban boards—things like the bug tracker and various spreadsheets for

Using Google Drawing as an Electronic "Wall"

At my company, Crisp, we wanted some kind of board to keep track of our consulting engagements and sales leads. We are rarely gathered in the same location, so a physical wall wouldn't work. We needed something electronic, yet we didn't want to sacrifice the flexibility of a wall.

Google Drawing turned out to be a great solution! It is just a drawing canvas. You can draw lines and rectangles, write text, and drag things around, just like on a physical whiteboard or wall. No constraints. And it's in the cloud, so everyone can see and update the board at the same time and see what is going on.

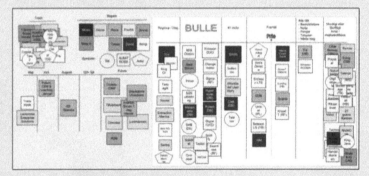

If we were collocated, we would definitely use a physical wall. But Google Drawing is the closest thing we've found to a wall for distributed organizations.

metrics and release planning. But the project board is the "master." We've all agreed to make sure that the board always reflects the truth and to keep it up-to-date in real time. Any other electronic docs that duplicate information on the board are considered to be "shadows" of the board—if things are out of sync, the board is always the master.

We have discussed introducing an electronic tool to duplicate parts of the board at a higher level. That way, we could automate some of the metrics and make a high-level electronic board visible to upper management and other stakeholders who aren't in the same physical location. It would cost some effort to keep the digital and physical boards in sync but might be worth it. This digital board, like our other electronic tools, would be a *complement* to the physical board, not a replacement. We haven't tried this yet, though.

As you can see, we're by no means at the end of our journey. There are always things that can be improved!

CHAPTER 16

What We Learned

Well, I think that concludes the case study. Hope you enjoyed the tour!

As you may have figured out, this case study is really all about organizational change! Here are some key takeaway points, from the perspective of a change agent (and anybody can be a change agent).

16.1 Know Your Goal

Get everyone together and agree on what "perfect" means in your context. What would a "perfect" process, organization, and work environment look like? This will just be your compass direction, so the goal doesn't have to be realistic. Perfection is a direction, not a place! Having a clearly defined direction makes it easier to focus and evaluate your improvement efforts.

16.2 Experiment

Don't look for perfect solutions. It's probably not worth the wait, and you'll probably get it wrong anyway. Instead, look for small incremental improvements, and think of them as *experiments*. An experiment may or may not lead to the intended improvement, but it should always generate insights that can be used to design the next experiment.

A great process isn't designed; it is *evolved*. So, the important thing isn't your process; the important thing is your process for *improving* your process.

16.3 Embrace Failure

Some changes just don't work out. Some changes even make things worse. Don't worry about it, because few failures are irreversible. Fear of failure is the biggest enemy of innovation. Instead of asking "Why did we fail? Who screwed up?" ask "What did we learn, and what will we try next?"

The only *real* failure is the failure to learn from failure.

16.4 Solve Real Problems

Whenever you're trying to change something, ask yourself continuously, "What problem am I trying to solve? Is it real or hypothetical? Is there any other more important problem that I should focus on instead?" When in doubt, ask people! It is very easy to fall into the trap of focusing on irrelevant or imagined problems, especially as external coach on a part-time basis.

16.5 Have Dedicated Change Agents

Change is hard! Especially when it involves people. And organizational change always involves people. One critical success factor is having at least one dedicated change agent, someone who focuses almost entirely on driving, leading, and facilitating the change process.

Even better, have two change agents: one insider and one outsider. The insider (typically an employee) has the domain knowledge, knows who to talk to for what, and knows the history of the organization and what has worked in the past. The outsider (typically a consultant) provides a fresh perspective and experience from helping other companies go through the same type of change.

Culture can be defined as "things that everyone does without noticing it." An outsider is more likely to notice, and challenge, the status quo.

16.6 Involve People

Most people like change; they just don't like to *be changed*. So, don't make any change without first involving the people who will be affected by it. Forcing people to change is usually ineffective, unnecessary, and, well, cruel. If people resist your great change proposal, you probably haven't made the problem clear enough. Or you're solving the wrong problem. Go back to your cause-effect diagram (see Chapter 20, *Cause-Effect Diagrams*, on page 131) and think again!

Better yet, don't even make the change proposal yourself. Instead, visualize the problem that you think you see, and engage the people affected by the problem to propose solutions. People are much more likely to accept a change if it was their own idea!

Once everyone agrees that the problem really *is* a problem and that it is worth solving, then you're halfway to the solution!

Part II

A Closer Look at the Techniques

Oh, did you want more? OK, let's go deeper into some of the techniques mentioned in this book.

CHAPTER 17

Agile and Lean in a Nutshell

Probably most people reading this book have a basic understanding of Agile and Lean principles, but this quick summary will remind those less familiar with the techniques and demonstrate how they tie in with the associated methods Scrum, XP, and Kanban.

Broadly speaking, Lean and Agile are two sets of highly compatible values and principles that outline how to succeed with product development. Scrum, XP, and Kanban are three concrete ways of putting these principles into practice. In other words, they are three slightly overlapping flavors of Lean and Agile software development.

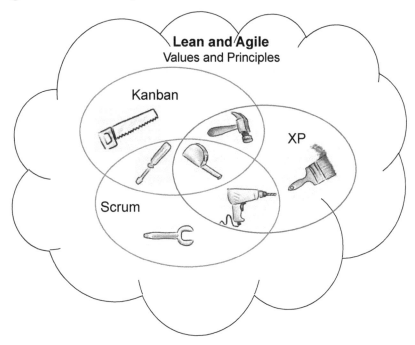

Scrum and XP and Kanban offer concrete techniques such as sprint planning meetings (Scrum), pair programming (XP), and limit work in progress (Kanban). These techniques can be seen as *process tools*. The three toolkits have significant overlap; for example, all three recommend the use of physical taskboards to visualize what is going on.

17.1 Agile in a Nutshell

The term *Agile software development* was coined in 2001, when seventeen thought leaders from the software community met at a ski resort in Utah to discuss and compare notes on how to succeed with software development. These people had independently been creating new methods such as Scrum, XP, and Dynamic Systems Development Method (DSDM). During the meeting, they discovered a strong common ground: a shared vision of how to succeed with software development. This became known as the Agile Manifesto.[1]

Here is the manifesto:

> We are uncovering better ways of developing software by doing it and helping others do it. Through this work we have come to value:
>
> - *Individuals and interactions* over processes and tools
>
> - *Working software* over comprehensive documentation

---

1.   www.agilemanifesto.org

- *Customer collaboration* over contract negotiation

- *Responding to change* over following a plan

That is, while there is value in the items on the right, we value the items on the left more.

After the meeting they agreed on twelve principles behind these values:

- Our highest priority is to satisfy the customer through early and continuous delivery of valuable software.

- Welcome changing requirements, even late in development. Agile processes harness change for the customer's competitive advantage.

- Deliver working software frequently, from a couple of weeks to a couple of months, with a preference to the shorter timescale.

- Businesspeople and developers must work together daily throughout the project.

- Build projects around motivated individuals. Give them the environment and support they need, and trust them to get the job done.

- The most efficient and effective method of conveying information to and within a development team is face-to-face conversation.

- Working software is the primary measure of progress.

- Agile processes promote sustainable development. The sponsors, developers, and users should be able to maintain a constant pace indefinitely.

- Continuous attention to technical excellence and good design enhances agility.

- Simplicity—the art of maximizing the amount of work not done—is essential.

- The best architectures, requirements, and designs emerge from self-organizing teams.

- At regular intervals, the team reflects on how to become more effective, then tunes and adjusts its behavior accordingly.

Although the term *Agile* was coined in 2001, most Agile methods were created in the 1980s and 1990s. Agile is just an umbrella term, a description of the common denominator. Any method or approach that follows these values and principles can be considered Agile.

The Agile Manifesto is a historical document, a call for change. The wording of the manifesto resonated deeply with thousands of people around the world, causing somewhat of a revolution in software development. Ten years later, all the authors (except one) met again in the same location and concluded that they still stand behind agile values and principles. So, it seems that, despite the fast pace of change in the software industry, the Agile Manifesto is standing the test of time.

Nobody owns the term *Agile software development*, so it has many interpretations. We know what Agile meant in 2001 (through the manifesto); today it is less clear. Many of the original manifesto authors hope that the term *Agile* will eventually fall out of use, signifying that the Agile values and principles have become simply "the way we do software."

17.2 Lean in a Nutshell

Lean is the western term for what the Japanese call "TPS" (Toyota Production System)—an approach to manufacturing that has helped make Toyota the most successful car manufacturer in the world. The underlying principles behind TPS, the Toyota Way, have turned out to be applicable almost anywhere, including software development.

Agile and Lean can be seen as cousins with common values but different origins. Lean arose from manufacturing. Agile arose from software development. Both sets of principles fit well together and are very broadly applicable. More and more software development organizations are discovering how to combine these principles to cover the whole chain from product concept to delivery.

Mary and Tom Poppendieck have been instrumental in mapping Lean principles to software development. Here is their summary.[2]

Optimize the Whole

Optimizing a part of a system will always, over time, suboptimize the overall system.

- *Focus on the entire value stream*: From concept to cash. From customer request to deployed software.

- *Deliver a complete product*: Customers don't want software; they want their problems solved. Complete solutions are built by complete teams.

- *Think long term*: Beware of governance and incentive systems that drive short-term thinking and optimize local performance.

---

2. www.poppendieck.com

Eliminate Waste

Waste is anything that does not add customer value. The three biggest wastes in software development are the following:

- *Building the wrong thing*: "There is nothing so useless as doing efficiently that which should not be done at all."

- *Failure to learn*: Many of our policies—for example, *governance by variance from plan, frequent handovers*, and *separating decision making from work*—interfere with the learning that is the essence of development.

- *Thrashing*: Practices that interfere with the smooth flow of value—task switching, long lists of requests, big piles of partly done work—deliver half the value for twice the effort.

Build Quality In

If you routinely find defects in your verification process, your process is defective.

- *Final verification should not find defects*: Every software development process ever invented had as its primary purpose finding and fixing defects as early in the development process as possible.

- *Mistake-proof your process with test-first development*: Tests—including unit tests, end-to-end tests, and integration tests—must be available to establish confidence in the correctness of the system at any time during development, at every level of the system.

- *Break dependencies*: System architecture should support the addition of any feature at any time.

Learn Constantly

Planning is useful. Learning is essential.

- *Predictable performance is driven by feedback*: A predictable organization does not guess about the future and call it a plan; it develops the capacity to rapidly respond to the future as it unfolds.

- *Maintain options*: Think of code as an experiment—make it change-tolerant.

- *Last responsible moment*: Learn as much as possible before making irreversible decisions. Don't make decisions that will be expensive to change before their time—and don't make them after their time!

Deliver Fast

Start with a deep understanding of all stakeholders and what they will value. Create a steady, even flow of work, pulled from this deep understanding of value.

- *Rapid delivery, high quality, and low cost are fully compatible*: Companies that compete on the basis of speed have a big cost advantage, deliver superior quality, and are more attuned to their customers' needs.

- *Queuing theory applies to development, not just servers*: Focusing on use creates traffic jams that reduce use. Drive down cycle time with small batches and fewer things in process. Aggressively limit the size of lists and queues.

- *Managing workflow is a lot easier than managing schedules*: The best way to establish reliable, predictable deliveries is to establish reliable, repeatable workflows with iterations or a Kanban system.

Engage Everyone

The time and energy of bright, creative people are the scarce resources in today's economy and the basis of competitive advantage.

People who are paid fairly and adequately are motivated by autonomy, mastery, and purpose.[3]

- *Autonomy*: The most effective work groups are semi-autonomous teams with an internal leader who has end-to-end responsibility for complete, meaningful tasks.

- *Mastery*: Respect for people means providing the challenge, feedback, and environment that enables everyone to become excellent.

- *Purpose*: Tie work to value. Only by believing in the purpose of their work will people become engaged in achieving that purpose.

Keep Getting Better

Results are not the point—the point is to develop the people and the systems capable of delivering results.

---

3.   http://www.youtube.com/watch?v=u6XAPnuFjJc

- *Failure is a learning opportunity*: The most reliable performance comes when even small failures are deeply investigated and corrected—when noise is not tolerated.

- *Standards exist to be challenged and improved*: Embody the current, best-known practice in standards that everyone follows, while encouraging everyone to challenge and change the standards.

- *Use the scientific method*: Teach teams to establish hypotheses, conduct many rapid experiments, create concise documentation, and implement the best alternative.

17.3 Scrum in a Nutshell

Scrum is a software development approach that Jeff Sutherland and Ken Schwaber developed during the early 1990s. It is rooted in empirical process control and complex adaptive systems theory and was inspired by a *Harvard Business Review* article called "New New Product Development Game" from 1986.[4]

The core concepts of Scrum are as follows.

Ordered Product Backlog

Split your work into a list of small, concrete deliverables—the *product backlog*. The product owner defines a product vision and orders the backlog by business value and other factors such as risk and dependencies.

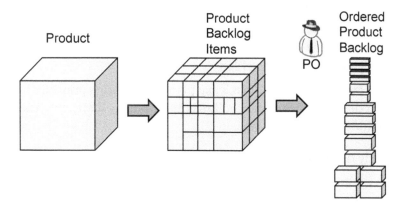

---

4.   http://hbr.org/product/new-new-product-development-game/an/86116-PDF-ENG

Cross-functional Teams

Split your organization into small, cross-functional, self-organizing teams. Each team has a product owner, who provides the vision and overall business priorities, and a Scrum master, who focuses on improving the team and removing impediments.

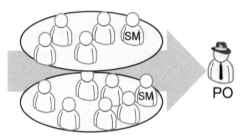

Sprints

Split time into short fixed-length iterations, or *sprints* (typically two or three weeks long). The team chooses how many product backlog items to pull into each iteration. Each iteration ends with a demonstration of a tested, potentially shippable release.

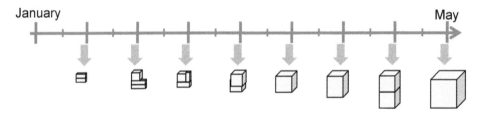

Continuously Adjusted Release Plan

The product owner optimizes the release plan and updates priorities in collaboration with the customer, based on insights gained by inspecting the release after each iteration.

Continuously Adjusted Process

The teams optimize the development process by having a retrospective after each iteration.

So, with Scrum:

Instead of a *large group* spending a *long time* building a *big thing*...

...we have a *small team* spending a *short time* building a *small thing*.

But *integrating regularly* to see the whole.

Scrum does not mandate any specific engineering practices—those are left up to the team. In practice, however, succeeding with Scrum *without* including the core engineering practices of XP is very hard.

17.4 XP in a Nutshell

Extreme Programming (XP) is a software development approach that Kent Beck created in the mid-1990s. It is based on the values of simplicity, communication, feedback, courage, and respect. XP evolved in parallel with Scrum and, in fact, includes most of the same elements. For example, *on-site customer* in XP corresponds roughly to *product owner* in Scrum.

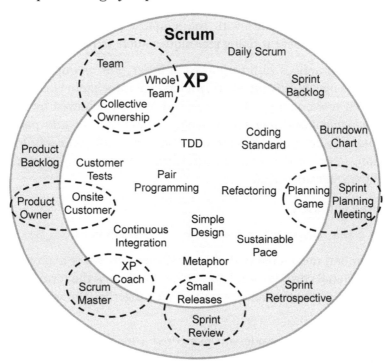

In that sense, Scrum can be seen as a "wrapper" around XP, focusing on structural issues and external communication, while XP duplicates most of that and adds some team-internal engineering practices. These include the following:

- *Continuous integration*: Have a system that automatically builds, integrates, and tests the code as the team develops it. This gives the team early feedback on the quality of their work.

- *Pair programming*: Program together in pairs on one workstation to maximize learning, maximize design quality, and minimize defects.

- *Test-driven development*: Use test code to drive the design of the system. Write an automated test, then write just enough code to make that one test pass, and then refactor the code primarily to improve readability and remove duplication. Rinse and repeat.

- *Collective code ownership*: Anybody on the team is allowed to (and, in fact, encouraged to) edit any part of the code base. This creates a sense of team ownership and ensures a coherent, easy-to-understand design across the whole system.

- *Incremental design improvement*: Instead of creating a complete design from the beginning, start with the simplest possible design and then continuously improve it using techniques such as refactoring.

Many of these practices build upon each other. For example, *incremental design improvement* is difficult, scary, and risky if the system isn't well covered by automated tests, and good test coverage is best achieved by doing *test-driven development* and *pair programming*. However, that gets painful if all the tests have to be triggered manually and run locally on each developer's workstation, so we need a *continuous integration* system to do that automatically in the background. And so on.

17.5 Kanban in a Nutshell

Kanban is a Lean approach to Agile software development.

Actually, Kanban means many things. Literally, Kanban is a Japanese word that means "visual card" (or sign). At Toyota, Kanban is the term used for the visual and physical signaling system that ties together the whole Lean production system.

In 2004, however, David Anderson pioneered a more direct implementation of Lean thinking and the Theory of Constraints[5] to software development. Under the guidance of experts such as Don Reinertsen, this evolved into what David called a "Kanban system for software development" and which most people now simply refer to as "Kanban."

So although Kanban as applied to software development is quite new, Kanban as used in Lean production is more than a half-century old.

---

5. http://en.wikipedia.org/wiki/Theory_of_Constraints

The rules of Kanban are simple. But, like chess, just because the rules are simple doesn't mean the game is easy.

- *Visualize the workflow*:

  - Split the work into pieces, write each item on a card, and put the card on the wall.

  - Use named columns to illustrate where each item is in the workflow.

- *Limit work in progress (WIP)*: Assign explicit limits to how many items may be in progress at each workflow state.

- *Measure and manage cycle time*: Average the time to complete one item, sometimes called *lead time* (a better term might be *flowthrough time*). Optimize the process to make the cycle time as small and predictable as possible.

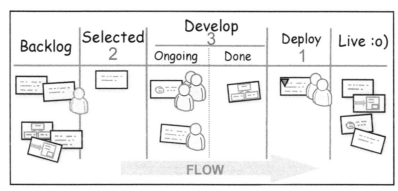

This is basically a direct implementation of a Lean pull-scheduling system.

While Scrum focuses on structure and communication and XP adds engineering practices, Kanban focuses on visualizing flow and managing bottlenecks.

One Day in Kanban Land

Here's a cartoon that illustrates the type of behavior that Kanban tries to drive:

Backlog
Selected
2
Develop
3
Ongoing
Done
Deploy
1
Live :o)
FLOW
Backlog
Selected
2
Develop
2
Ongoing
Done
Deploy
1
Live!
A
B
G
C
F
D
A & B are the 2 most important things right now!
Backlog
Selected
2
Develop
2
Ongoing
Done
Deploy
1
Live!
A
We'll do A
B
And we'll do B
G
F
C
H
I
D
Great! Next is C & D!
Backlog
Selected
2
Develop
2
Ongoing
Done
Deploy
1
Live!
A is done!
A
Hmmm... might need J+K+L as well
B
C
D
H
I
K
J
L
Ah, something to deploy!

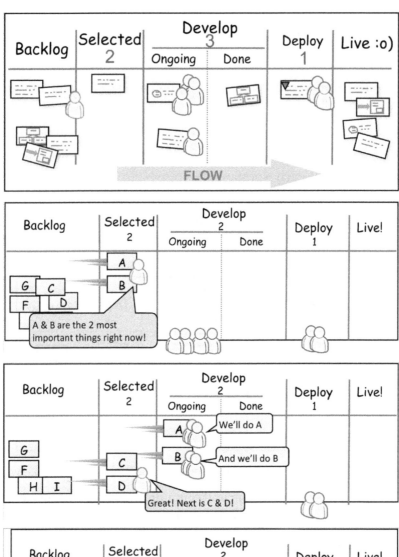

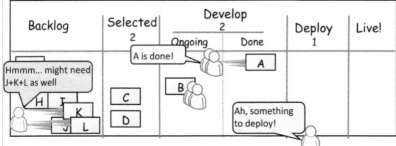

Backlog
Selected
2
Developing C!
Develop
2
Ongoing
Done
Deploy
1
Live!
Deploying A!
G
F
H
I
K
J
L
D
C
B
A
Backlog
Selected
2
Develop
2
Ongoing
Done
Deploy
1
Live!
B is done!
Crap! A doesn't build!
G
F
H
I
K
J
L
D
C
B
A
Backlog
Selected
2
Develop
2
Ongoing
Done
Deploy
1
Live!
We'll do D! No, wait.... that would break the Kanban limit of 2!
G
F
H
I
K
J
L
D
C
B
A
Backlog
Selected
2
Develop
2
Ongoing
Done
Deploy
1
Live!
K is pretty urgent. I'll schedule it next.
G
F
H
I
K
D
J
L
C
B
A
How can we help?
Get coffee. Then tell us what this #%&@ stack trace means.

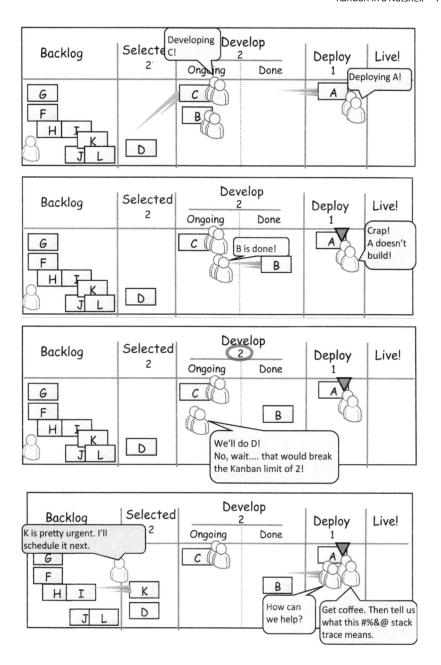

Backlog
Selected 2
Develop 2
Ongoing
Done
Deploy 1
Live!
G
F
H I
J L
K
D
C
B
A
C is done!
Great, hope you start K soon!
Sure, as soon as we sort out the problem with A.
Backlog
Selected 2
Develop 2
Ongoing
Done
Deploy 1
Live!
How can we help?
I want F & G as well. But the Kanban limit stops me. Hmmm....
We don't need any more hands right now. But this is a recurring problem, so write a test for it to avoid the problem in the future!
Backlog
Selected 2
Develop 2
Ongoing
Done
Deploy 1
Live!
G
F
H I
J L
K
D
C
B
A
Is there anything I can do to help? I'm no techie but...
Sure! Get more coffee and protect us from disruptions.
A few days later...
Backlog
Selected 2
Develop 3
Ongoing
Done
Deploy 1
Live!
M
H
L
J
R
I
G
F
D
K
A
B
C
M or H. Definitely M!
No, H! Hmmmmm. No wait, M!
M or H or M or H?!? Aaaaarrrrgh
Don't you miss the old days?
All-night Integration hell?
Big-bang releases?
LOL

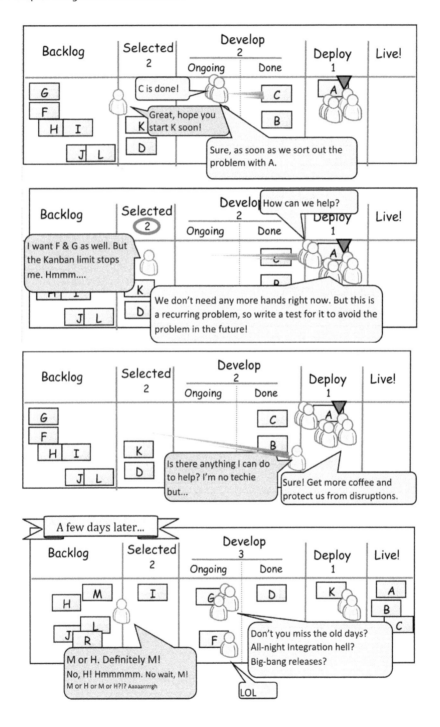

CHAPTER 18

Reducing the Test Automation Backlog

Many companies with existing legacy code bases bump into a huge impediment when they want to get Agile: lack of test automation!

Without test automation, making changes in the system is very hard, because things break without anybody noticing. When the new release goes live, the real users discover the defects, causing embarrassment and an expensive hotfix—or even worse, a chain of hotfixes, because each hotfix introduces new, unanticipated defects.

This makes the team terribly afraid to change code and therefore reluctant to improve the design of the code, which leads to a downward spiral of worse and worse code as the system grows.

The good news is that you can do something about it!

18.1 What to Do About It

Your main options in this case are as follows:

- Ignore the problem. Let the system decline into entropy death, and hope that nobody needs it by then.

- Rebuild the system from scratch using test-driven development to ensure good test coverage.

- Start a separate test automation project, where a dedicated team improves the test coverage for the system until it's adequate.

- Let the team improve test coverage a little bit each iteration.

Guess which approach usually works best? Yep, the last one—improve test coverage a little bit each iteration. At least in my experience.

The third option may sound tempting, but it's risky. Who's going to do the test automation? A separate team? If so, does that mean the other developers don't need to learn how to automate tests? That's a problem. Or is the whole team doing the test automation project? In that case, their velocity (from a business perspective) is 0 until they're done. So, when are they done? When does test automation "end"?

Let's get back to the fourth option—improve test coverage a little bit each iteration. So, how to do that in practice?

18.2 How to Improve Test Coverage a Little Bit Each Iteration

Here's an approach that I like:

1. List your test cases.

2. Classify each test by risk, how expensive it is to do manually, and how expensive it is to automate.

3. Sort the list in priority order.

4. Automate a few tests each iteration, starting from the highest priority.

So, let's take a look at each of these steps.

18.3 Step 1: List Your Test Cases

Think about how you test your system today. Brainstorm a list of your most important test cases—the ones that you already execute manually today or wish you had time to execute. Here's an example from a hypothetical online banking system:

Test Case
Change Skin
Security Alert
Transaction History
Block Account
Add New User
Sort Query Results
Deposit Cash
Validate Transfer

18.4 Step 2: Classify Each Test

First classify your test cases by risk. Look at your list of tests. Ignore the cost of manual testing for the moment. Now, what if you could throw away half of the tests and never execute them? Which tests would you keep? This factor is a combination of the probability of failure and the cost of failure.

Highlight the risky tests, the ones that keep you awake at night.

Test Case	Risk
Change Skin	
Security Alert	
Transaction History	
Block Account	
Add New User	
Sort Query Results	
Deposit Cash	
Validate Transfer	

Now think about how long each test takes to execute manually. Which half of the tests takes the longest? Highlight those.

Test Case	Risk	Manual Test Cost
Change Skin		
Security Alert		
Transaction History		
Block Account		
Add New User		
Sort Query Results		
Deposit Cash		
Validate Transfer		

Finally, think about how much work it would be to write automation scripts for each test. Highlight the most expensive half.

Test Case	Risk	Pay Every Time! Manual Test Cost	Pay Only Once! Automation Cost
Change Skin			
Security Alert			
Transaction History			
Block Account			
Add New User			
Sort Query Results			
Deposit Cash			
Validate Transfer			

Note that *manual test cost* is incurred every time the test is run, while *automation cost* is incurred only once. So, time spent writing test automation code is actually an investment, not a cost.

18.5 Step 3: Sort the List in Priority Order

Which test do you think we should automate first? Should we automate *Change skin*, which is low-risk, easy to test manually, and difficult to automate? Or should we automate *Block account*, which is high-risk, difficult to test manually, and easy to automate? That's a fairly easy decision.

Here's a more difficult decision. Should we automate *Validate transfer*, which is high-risk, hard to test manually, and hard to automate? Or should we automate *Deposit cash*, which also is high-risk but easy to test manually and easy to automate? That decision is context dependent.

You basically need to make three decisions about which test to automate first:

- The high-risk test that's easy to test manually or the low-risk test that's difficult to test manually

- The test that's easy to do manually and easy to automate or the test that's hard to do manually and hard to automate

- The high-risk test that's hard to automate or the low-risk test that's easy to automate

Those decisions give you a prioritization of your categories, which in turn lets you sort your list of test cases by priority. In my example, I decided to prioritize manual test cost first, then risk, then automation cost. Here's the sorted list:

So, that's it! A prioritized backlog of test automation stories.

Of course, we could also invent some kind of calculation algorithm. For example, we could give each highlighted cell one point. Then we just add up each row and sort. Or we could just sort the list manually using gut feel.

We could also use more precise units such as hours and story points for each category:

Test Case	Risk	Manual Test Cost	Automation Cost
Block Account	High	5 hrs	0.5 sp
Validate Transfer	High	3 hrs	1 sp
Transaction History	Medium	3 hrs	1 sp
Sort Query Results	Medium	2 hrs	8 sp
Deposit Cash	High	1.5 hr	1 sp
Security Alert	High	1 hr	13 sp
Add New User	Low	0.5 hr	3 sp
Change Skin	Low	0.5 hr	20 sp

Remember, though, that our goal for the moment is just to prioritize the list. If we can do that with a simple and crude categorization scheme, then there's no need to complicate things, right? Analysis is useful, but over-analysis is a waste of time.

Anyway, now we have a prioritized test automation backlog!

18.6 Step 4: Automate a Few Tests Each Iteration

Regardless of the test automation backlog, each *new* feature should include an automated test at the feature level. That's the XP practice known as *customer acceptance tests*. Not doing that is what got your system into this mess in the first place.

But in addition to implementing new stories, we want to spend some time automating old test cases for previously existing stories. How much time should we spend on that? The team needs to negotiate that with the product owner.

For example, we may agree that 80 percent of the team's capacity will be spent on developing new features from the product backlog and 20 percent of the capacity will be spent on the test automation backlog. So, during each iteration planning meeting, the team will pull from both backlogs.

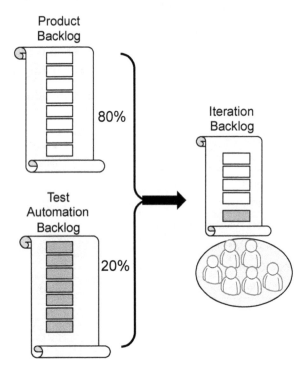

Here are some other examples of how the agreement might look:

- In each iteration we will implement one test automation story.

- In each iteration we will implement up to ten story points of test automation stories.

- In each iteration we will finish the product backlog stories first and then spend the remainder of the time (if any) implementing test automation stories.

- The product owner will merge the test automation stories into the overall product backlog, and the team will treat them just like any other story.

The exact form of the agreement doesn't matter. You can change it every iteration if you like (as long as the team and product owner agree). The important thing is that the test automation debt is gradually repaid, step by step.

After finishing half the stories on your test automation backlog, you might decide, "Hey, we've paid back enough debt now! Let's just skip the rest of the old test cases; they're not worth automating anyway," and dump the rest. In that case, congratulations!

18.7 Does This Solve the Problem?

Following this pattern does not magically solve your test automation problem, at least not in the short term. However, this pattern does make the problem easier to approach. Within a few months you should notice a significant difference.

CHAPTER 19

Sizing the Backlog with Planning Poker

Planning Poker is a simple but powerful tool that makes team estimating (that is, estimating the effort involved in building a feature) faster, more accurate, and more fun. The term was coined by James Grenning and popularized by Mike Cohn.

19.1 Estimating Without Planning Poker

Here's a typical problem with team estimates. Let's say we're in a sprint planning meeting, and the product owner says....

OK guys, how big is this feature?

So, the team starts thinking about how big the feature is.

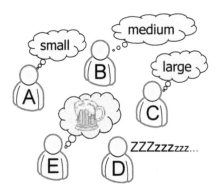

Mr. A believes that he knows exactly what needs to be done, and it isn't much work at all. Mrs. B and C are more pessimistic. Mr. D and E are slacking off. So, Mr. A says....

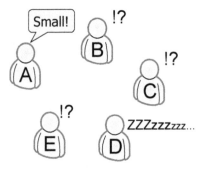

This makes B and C confused. They start doubting their own estimates. Mr. E wakes up and doesn't really know what is being estimated. D is still dozing.

The product owner asks for the rest of the team's estimates.

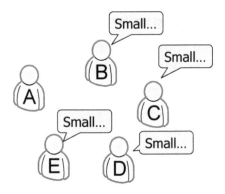

As you can see, the rest of the team has been heavily influenced by A, just because A spoke up first. We have lost the opportunity to hear why Mrs. B and Mrs. C think this is a medium to large feature, which may be valuable information!

19.2 Estimating with Planning Poker

Now imagine that each team member is holding the following cards. (Our Planning Poker cards actually use numbers: 1 to symbolize Small, 2 to symbolize Medium, and 3 to symbolize Large.)

Let's redo the estimate. The product owner says....

Once again, the team starts thinking about how big the feature is.

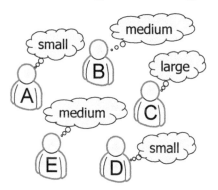

This time nobody blurts anything out. Instead, they all have to present a card, face down, that represents their estimate. Everybody has to present a card, so Mr. D and E wake up. Mr. D admits that he was sleeping and asks what the feature is about. It's harder to slack off when doing estimates this way!

When they're done, all cards are turned over simultaneously, revealing everyone's estimates.

Whoops! Big divergence here. The team, in particular Mr. A and Mrs. C, needs to discuss this feature and why their estimates are so wildly different. After some discussion, Mr. A realizes that he forgot some important tasks that need to be included in the feature. Mrs. C realizes that, with the design that Mr. A presented, the feature might not be so large after all.

After the discussion (three minutes in total), they do another estimation round for that same feature.

Convergence! OK, not complete convergence. But they agree that Medium should be an OK estimate. Next feature.

19.3 Special Cards

 The question mark card means, "I have absolutely no idea at all. That feature might be huge, or it might be tiny." This circumstance should be rare. If this card is used too often, the team needs to discuss the features more and try to achieve a better knowledge spread within the team.

 The coffee cup card means, "I'm too tired to think. Let's take a short break!"

> **Joe asks:**
> ## Won't All Features Average Out to Medium Whenever Estimates Diverge?
>
> No, not if the team has a discussion about *why* there is divergence and then plays another round based on that information. One person may convince the rest of the team that this feature is Small, because it has already been implemented in another system and can be reused. Or vice versa—one person may convince the rest of the team that this feature is Large, because of some risk that nobody else thought of.

Most teams like Planning Poker because it takes much of the pain out of estimating and instead turns it into a simple and fun process. The greatest value is really in the conversations that get triggered while playing; the estimate itself is just a positive side effect.

CHAPTER 20

Cause-Effect Diagrams

Cause-effect diagrams are a simple and pragmatic way of doing root-cause analysis. I've been using these diagrams for years to help organizations understand and solve all kinds of problems, technical as well as organizational.

Let's take a closer look at how cause-effect diagrams work so you can put them to use in your own context.

20.1 Solve Problems, Not Symptoms

The key to effective problem solving is first to make sure you understand the problem you are trying to solve—why it needs to be solved, how you'll know when you've solved it, and what the root cause of it is.

Symptoms often show up in one place, while the cause of the problem is somewhere else. If you "solve" the symptom without digging deeper, it's highly likely that the problem will just reappear later in a different shape. Let's look at a couple of examples.

- *Problem*: Smoke in my bedroom.

    - *Bad solution*: Open the window and go back to sleep.
    - *Good solution*: Find the source of the smoke and solve it. Whoops, there's a fire in the basement! Extinguish it, find out what caused the fire in the first place, and install a fire alarm for earlier warning next time.

- *Problem*: Hot forehead, tired.

    - *Bad solution*: Put ice on forehead to cool it down. Drink some coffee to wake up. Keep working.
    - *Good solution*: Take my temperature. Oh, I have fever! Go home and rest.

- *Problem*: Memory leak in server.

  - *Bad solution*: Buy more memory.
  - *Good solution*: Find and fix the source of the memory leak. Implement tests to detect new memory leaks in the future.

- *Problem*: Water in the boat.

  - *Bad solution*: Pump out the water and keep sailing.
  - *Good solution*: Find the source of the water. Ah, a hole! Fix it. Then pump out the water.

...and so on.

Most problems in organizations are systemic. The "system" (your organization) has a glitch that needs to be fixed. Until you find the source of the glitch, most attempts to fix the problem will be futile or even counterproductive.

20.2 The Lean Problem-Solving Approach: A3 Thinking

One of the core tenets of Lean thinking is Kaizen—continuous process improvement. Toyota attributes much of its success to its highly disciplined problem-solving approach. This approach is sometimes called A3 thinking (based on the single A3-size papers used to capture knowledge from each problem-solving effort).

You can download an A3 example and template from http://www.crisp.se/lean/a3-template. It is hard to show here because, well, A3 is probably a lot larger than what you are holding in your hand right now. Figure 2, *A3 Example*, on page 133 shows a high-level view, though.

With the A3 approach, a significant amount of time (the left half of the sheet) is spent analyzing and visualizing the root cause of a problem before proposing solutions. A cause-effect diagram is only one way of doing a root-cause analysis. There are other ways, too, such as value stream maps and Ishikawa (fishbone) diagrams. This sample A3 contains a value stream map (top left) and a cause-effect diagram (bottom-left).

The nice thing about cause-effect diagrams is that they are fairly intuitive and self-explanatory (especially compared to fishbone diagrams). Another advantage is that you can illustrate reinforcing loops (vicious cycles), which is very useful from a systems-thinking perspective.

Let's look at how to create and use these diagrams effectively.

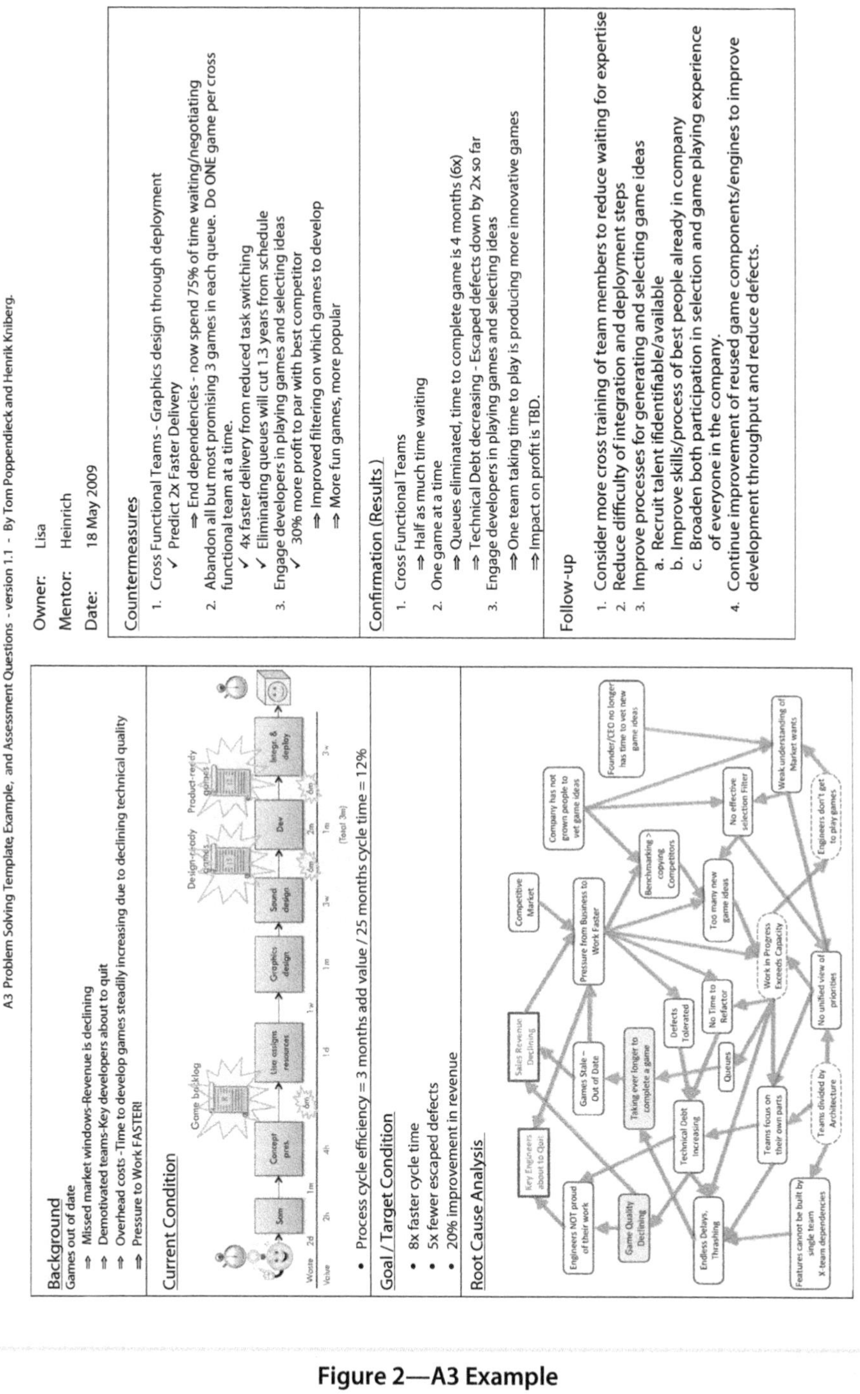

A3 Problem Solving Template, Example, and Assessment Questions - version 1.1 - By Tom Poppendieck and Henrik Kniberg.

Background

Games out of date

⇒ Missed market windows-Revenue is declining
⇒ Demotivated teams-Key developers about to quit
⇒ Overhead costs -Time to develop games steadily increasing due to declining technical quality
⇒ Pressure to Work FASTER!

Current Condition

Game backlog
Design-ready games
Product-ready games
Som
Concept pres.
Use assigns resources
Graphics design
Sound design
Dev
Integr. & deploy
Waste 2d 1m 6m 1w 6m 2m 6m
Value 2h 4h 1d 1m 3w 1m 3w
(Total 3m)

- Process cycle efficiency = 3 months add value / 25 months cycle time = 12%

Goal / Target Condition

- 8x faster cycle time
- 5x fewer escaped defects
- 20% improvement in revenue

Root Cause Analysis

Key Engineers about to Quit
Sales Revenue Declining
Competitive Market
Engineers NOT proud of their work
Games Stale – Out of Date
Pressure from Business to Work Faster
Company has not grown people to vet game ideas
Founder/CEO no longer has time to vet new game ideas
Game Quality Declining
Taking ever longer to complete a game
Benchmarking > copying Competitors
Defects Tolerated
Technical Debt Increasing
Endless Delays, Thrashing
Queues
No Time to Refactor
Too many new game ideas
No effective selection Filter
Teams focus on their own parts
Work in Progress Exceeds Capacity
Weak understanding of Market wants
Features cannot be built by single team X-team dependencies
Teams divided by Architecture
No unified view of priorities
Engineers don't get to play games

Owner: Lisa
Mentor: Heinrich
Date: 18 May 2009

Countermeasures

1. Cross Functional Teams - Graphics design through deployment
   ✓ Predict 2x Faster Delivery
   ⇒ End dependencies - now spend 75% of time waiting/negotiating
2. Abandon all but most promising 3 games in each queue. Do ONE game per cross functional team at a time.
   ✓ 4x faster delivery from reduced task switching
   ✓ Eliminating queues will cut 1.3 years from schedule
3. Engage developers in playing games and selecting ideas
   ✓ 30% more profit to par with best competitor
   ⇒ Improved filtering on which games to develop
   ⇒ More fun games, more popular

Confirmation (Results)

1. Cross Functional Teams
   ⇒ Half as much time waiting
2. One game at a time
   ⇒ Queues eliminated, time to complete game is 4 months (6x)
   ⇒ Technical Debt decreasing - Escaped defects down by 2x so far
3. Engage developers in playing games and selecting ideas
   ⇒ One team taking time to play is producing more innovative games
   ⇒ Impact on profit is TBD.

Follow-up

1. Consider more cross training of team members to reduce waiting for expertise
2. Reduce difficulty of integration and deployment steps
3. Improve processes for generating and selecting game ideas
   a. Recruit talent ifidentifiable/available
   b. Improve skills/process of best people already in company
   c. Broaden both participation in selection and game playing experience of everyone in the company.
4. Continue improvement of reused game components/engines to improve development throughput and reduce defects.

Figure 2—A3 Example

20.3 How to Use Cause-Effect Diagrams

Here's the basic process:

1. Select a problem—anything that's bothering you—and write it down.

2. Trace "upward" to figure out the business consequences, the "visible damage" that your problem is causing.

3. Trace "downward" to find the root cause (or causes).

4. Identify and highlight vicious cycles (circular paths).

5. Iterate these steps a few times to refine and clarify your diagram.

6. Decide which root causes to address and how (that is, which countermeasures to implement).

Later, follow up. If your countermeasures worked, congratulations! If your countermeasures didn't work, don't despair. Analyze why they didn't work, update your diagram based on the new knowledge gained, and try some other countermeasures.

A countermeasure is an experiment, not a solution. Your hypothesis is that this countermeasure will solve (or mitigate) the problem, but you can never be sure. In effect, you're prodding your system to see how it reacts. That's why the follow-up is important.

Failure really just means that your system is trying to tell you something—so you'd better listen. The only real failure is the failure to learn from failure!

20.4 Example 1: Long Release Cycle

Let's say our problem is that we always miss deadlines. More specifically, our releases always occur at a later date than planned.

```
┌─────────────────┐
│    Delayed      │
│    Releases     │
└─────────────────┘
```

A problem is a problem only if it conflicts with your goal. So, start by defining your goal, and think about the consequences of this problem in terms of your goal. This can be done by asking a series of "so what?" questions until you identify the visible damage.

Let's say our goal is to delight our customers and maximize our revenue. Our dialogue might sound something like this:

> **Lisa:** Who cares if the releases are delayed? What's the consequence?
>
> **Jim:** Delays make our release cycles long.
>
> **Lisa:** So what?
>
> **Jim:** That delays our revenues, which messes up our cash flow. It also causes us to lose customers, since they're impatient and don't like waiting longer than necessary!

As we talk, we add boxes and cause-effect arrows to the diagram. Normally I try to go "upward" from the original problem statement when mapping out consequences, but that isn't a strict rule.

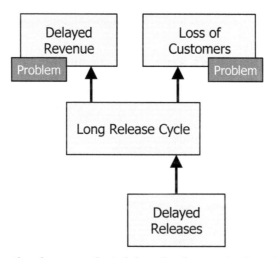

We can see from the diagram that delayed releases isn't really the problem. The *real* problem is delayed revenue and loss of customers. At this point we should consider three things:

- Are any *other* issues causing loss of customers or delayed revenues? If so, are delayed releases the biggest culprit, or should we turn our attention elsewhere?

- Can we quantify the problem? How much revenue have we lost? How many customers have we lost? This data will help us evaluate how much effort it's worth spending to solve this problem.

- How will we know when we've solved the problem? If a consultant comes in, does a noisy rain dance, and then proudly proclaims, "I've solved the problem now," how will we call the bluff?

Once we've spent some time analyzing the consequences of the problem, it's time to dig downward, toward the root.

First, ask a series of "why" questions. Yes, this is the "five whys" technique that you've probably heard of if you've studied Lean thinking.

Lisa: *Why are the releases delayed?*

Jim: *Because the scope keeps increasing.*

Lisa: *Why?*

Jim: *Because the customers come up with new features and insist that we add them to the current release, and they refuse to allow us to remove lower-priority features.*

Lisa: *Why? Why not defer the features until the next release?*

Jim: *Because the release cycle is so long, new demands appear before the release is done!*

OK, that was only three whys. But you get the picture.

The dialogue between Jim and Lisa gives us this next diagram:

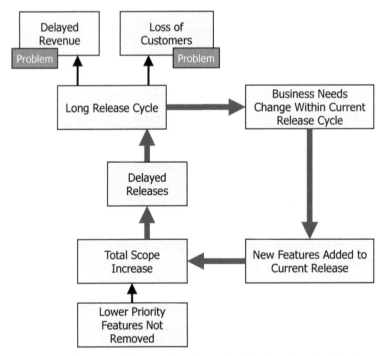

The vicious cycle (or reenforcing loop) is highlighted with thicker arrows. Recurring problems almost always involve loops like this, but they may take some time to find. Spotting these will greatly increase your likelihood of solving the problem effectively and permanently!

Our goal is to identify the root cause(s) of this problem, so we can achieve maximum effect with minimum effort. It's easy to miss important causes on the first pass, so go back and ask a few more whys.

Lisa: *Why is the release cycle so long? Are delayed releases the only cause?*

Jim: *Well, actually, even without the delays, our planned release cycles are quite long.*

Lisa: *How long is your planned release cycle?*

Jim: *Once per quarter.*

Lisa: *Why so long, then?*

Jim: *Because releases are expensive and complicated.*

Lisa: *Why?*

Jim: *Because there's so much stuff in each release, and it's all manual work.*

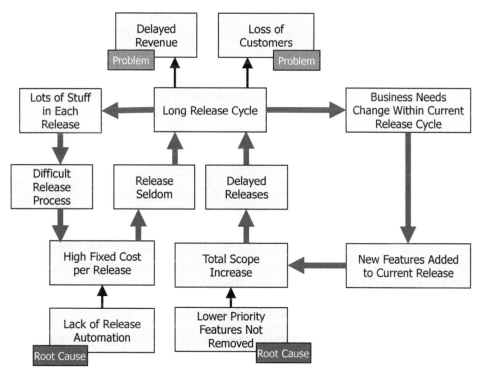

Look to the left—another vicious cycle (thick arrows)! The long time between releases means lots of stuff in each release, which means releases are difficult and expensive, which makes us reluctant to have frequent releases.

As you see, I've decided to label two root causes. Now it's time to propose countermeasures.

Root Cause	Countermeasure
Lack of release automation	Implement release automation
Lower-priority features not removed	Negotiate a rule with the customer, allowing them to add new features to a release only if they remove lower-priority features of corresponding size

There's no strict rule for determining which issue is the root cause, but here are some indicators:

- This issue has arrows only going out and no arrows coming in.

- It doesn't feel meaningful to dig further down (ask further "why" questions) from here.

- This issue is something we can address, and it will probably have a positive effect on the problem.

The *five whys* technique is called that because it typically takes about five "why" questions to get to the root. We tend to stop asking too early, so keep digging!

Note that the problem that was originally identified—delayed releases—wasn't really a problem or a root cause. It was just a symptom. We used that as a handle to dig upward to identify the real problem and then downward to identify the root causes. This system allows us to propose effective countermeasures in an informed way.

Without this type of analysis, we tend to jump to conclusions and execute ineffective and counterproductive changes—for example, adding more people, even though head count had nothing to do with the problem. Or changing the incentive model (reward people for releasing on time or punish people for releasing late), even though the current incentive model had nothing to do with the problem. I bet you've already seen that happen a few times.

20.5 Example 2: Defects Released to Production

Let's say that we're having problems with defective code being released to production.

```
┌─────────────┐
│   Defects   │
│ Released to │
│ Production  │
└─────────────┘
```

Lisa: So what?

Jim: The defects make our customers angry!

Lisa: Why are defects released to production?

Jim: Because they aren't properly tested before release.

Lisa: Why not?

...and so on. Here's where we ended up:

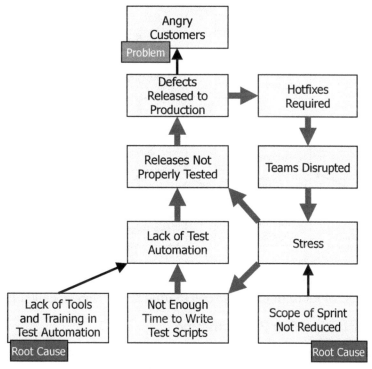

Look at that, two reinforcing loops! Check out the red arrows.

Loop 1 (inner loop): Defects in the product cause hotfixes, which disrupts the teams. Since teams aren't allowed to reduce the scope of the project, people get stressed and don't have time to test new releases properly. And that, of course, leads to more defects in production.

Loop 2 (outer loop): Because people are stressed, they don't have time to write automated test scripts, either. This leads to an overall lack of test automation, making it harder and harder to regression-test new releases properly, which leads to defects in production, more hotfixes, and ultimately more stress.

But wait, there's more!

Teams hate being disrupted. This disturbs flow and, in the long run, ruins motivation. This might explain why the staff turnover rate has been high! So in solving the original problem (defects in production), we get the added bonus of reducing team turnover!

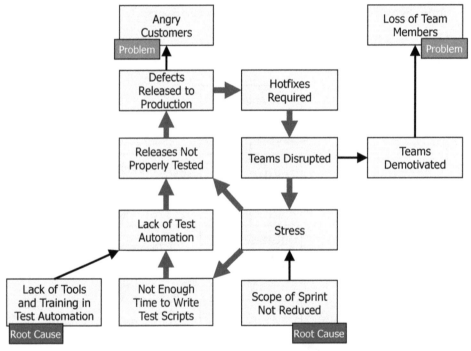

That's the nice thing about addressing the root cause. Root causes are usually the cause of more than one problem (that's why they're called *root*).

20.6 Example 3: Lack of Pair Programming

I was asked to help a client figure out why they weren't doing XP practices such as pair programming and test-driven development. "We know that we should be doing it, but we aren't," the client said.

So is lack of test-driven development (TDD) and pair programming really a problem? As usual, the things we call problems often turn out to be just symptoms.

Lisa: *What is the consequence of not doing pair programming and TDD?*

Jim: *We think we'd have much better code quality if we did these things.*

Lisa: *What is the consequence of bad code quality? Have you encountered any actual problems due to bad code quality?*

Jim: *Yeah, we've had some crashing demos. We're a research company, and demos are how we get business, so this really is a problem.*

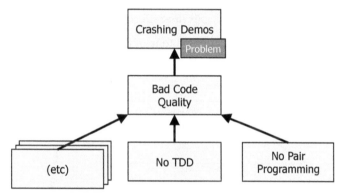

Let's take one of the issues and see whether we can dig down to the root.

Lisa: *Why aren't you pair programming, then?*

Jim: *Because many people are afraid that it won't work and we'll be wasting our time. We have no proof that it works.*

Lisa: *What kind of proof would you need?*

Jim: *Well, we've seen studies that indicate that it works. But nobody here has tried it, so we aren't sure that it works.*

There's the first loop:

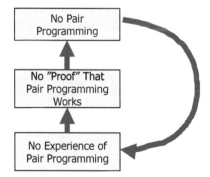

They don't want to do it because they don't know that it will work. And they don't know that it will work because they haven't tried it.

Lisa: *Why haven't you at least given pair programming a try?*

Jim: *We don't have time to experiment.*

Lisa: *Why not?*

Jim: *Because we don't have any slack. Each hour is accounted for. Our customers keep piling work on us.*

Lisa: *Why don't they let you manage your own time and let you pull in more work whenever you're ready?*

Jim: *They don't trust us to use our time effectively.*

The lack of trust also leads to a general fear of failure, which of course reduces the likelihood that they'll try something new like pair programming without "proof" that it works.

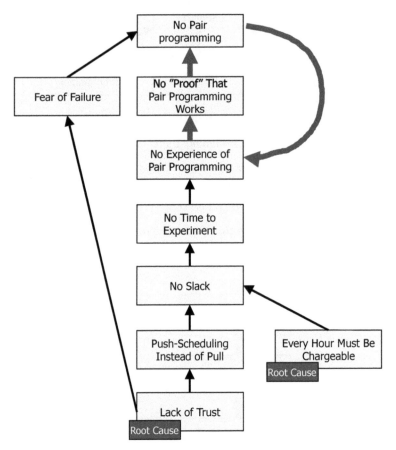

There appears to be two big root causes: lack of trust, and the management principle that every hour must be chargeable. Let's fold this back into the big picture.

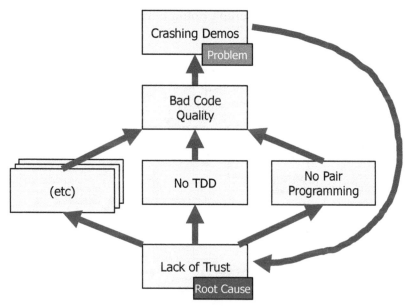

Lack of trust turned out to be the root cause of not doing XP practices such as TDD and pair programming, which caused bad quality, which caused crashing demos. And guess what? Crashing demos reduced trust even further. There's a vicious circle for you!

We did these exercises in a two-day workshop with about twenty-five people. At the beginning, we talked mostly about technical stuff—how to get started with TDD and pair programming. That didn't really get us anywhere, so we instead split into groups and had each group choose one problem, draw cause-effect diagrams, and create problem-solving A3s. The interesting thing was that several of the groups that analyzed seemingly different problems came up with the same root cause: lack of trust! This last diagram was just one example of that.

By the end of the day we were all talking about what we could do to increase the level of trust between the customer and the developers, which was a surprising turn of events.

For starters, we agreed that we should invite "them" (the customers) to participate the next time we do this type of workshop. That should lessen the use of terms like "us" and "them."

20.7 Example 4: Lots of Problems

Here's a bigger example. This organization was doing Scrum but was having some problems. The cause-effect diagram that emerged after interviews and workshops showed that they weren't doing Scrum correctly, and this was causing the problems.

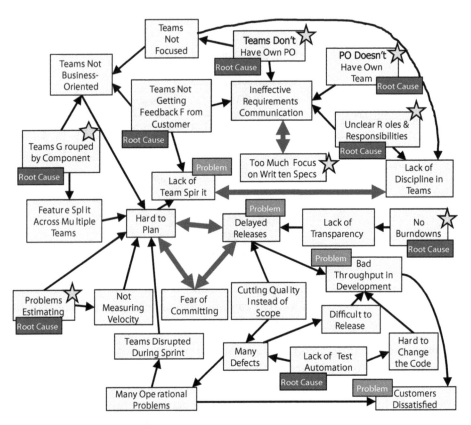

It became clear to everyone that many of the root causes could be addressed with a "proper" Scrum implementation (for example, reorganizing into cross-functional teams and making sure each team had a dedicated product owner). This triggered organizational changes that ultimately fixed many of the root causes (green stars). The next step was to improve test automation.

Scrum isn't always the solution, of course. In fact, sometimes Scrum itself is the problem, and other techniques such as Kanban are the solution. For more details on how Scrum and Kanban fit together, see *Kanban and Scrum—making the most of both* [KS09].

20.8 Practical Issues: How to Create and Maintain the Diagrams

So, how do we actually create the diagram? Well, that depends a bit on how many people are involved.

Working Alone

When creating the diagrams alone, I find it easiest to work directly with a diagramming tool such as Visio or PowerPoint. It's nice to be able to move things around quickly, resize the boxes, and make quick backups when playing around with the picture.

Working in a Small Group (2–8 People)

Gather in front of a whiteboard or flipchart. Use sticky notes for issues, and draw arrows to connect them. A whiteboard is preferable, so you could erase and redraw the arrows as you move the sticky notes around. Make sure everybody is helping out, not just one person doing all the drawing. Make sure someone takes a high-resolution photo and sends it to everyone after the meeting.

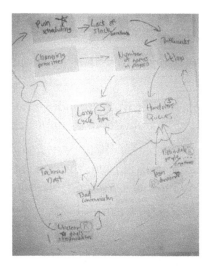

Working in a Larger Group (9–30 People)

Split the group into smaller teams, each focused around one specific problem. It's OK to have multiple teams working independently on the same problem—they may come to the same conclusion or different conclusions, and both cases are interesting. Each team works with a flipchart/whiteboard and sticky notes. Gather everyone together at regular intervals to share insights.

Long-Term Maintenance of a Diagram

Let the diagram live in a tool such as Visio or PowerPoint. Whenever you get to a workshop setting, decide whether the meeting is mostly for presenting the diagram or for updating it. If presenting, use a projector to show the diagram directly in Visio (or whatever tool you use). If updating the picture, replicate it on a whiteboard/flipchart with sticky notes and arrows so that people can collaborate effectively. Then synchronize with the electronic tool after the meeting.

This type of synchronizing does take some time, but it's often worth it. Nothing can beat physical tools like whiteboards and sticky notes when doing team workshops.

20.9 Pitfalls

Let's look at some typical pitfalls when creating these diagrams and how to avoid them.

Too Many Arrows and Boxes

Sometimes a helpful diagram can turn into a rat's maze. In that case, you need to simplify it. Here are some techniques:

- Remove redundant boxes (boxes that don't add much value to the diagram).

- Focus on "depth first" rather than "breadth first." Don't write down all causes of a problem; write only the most important one or two, and then keep digging deeper.

- Accept imperfections: a diagram like this will never be perfect. George Box puts it nicely: "All models are wrong, but some are useful."

- Maybe your problem area is too broad. Try to limit yourself to a more narrowly defined problem.

- Split the diagram into pieces, like I did in the previous example 3.

Oversimplification

This type of cause-effect diagram is simple, intentionally so. It doesn't replace face-to-face communication. If you need something more advanced or formally defined, read a book on systems thinking such as *The Fifth Discipline* [Sen94]. There are ways to distinguish between reinforcing loops and balancing loops and ways of adding a temporal dimension (showing how X causes Y but with a delay). Just beware: even a "perfect" diagram is useless if you need a doctoral degree to understand it.

Getting Personal

Avoid "blame game" issues such as the following:

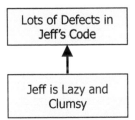

Problem solving works best if you assume that all problems are systemic. Sure, some people are clumsy. But even if that causes us significant problems, that's still a systemic problem—we have a system that assumes clumsy people aren't clumsy, a system that lets extremely clumsy people in, or a system that doesn't help clumsy people get less clumsy, and so on.

20.10 Why Use Cause-Effect Diagrams?

In summary, cause-effect diagrams are a great way to help teams:

- *Create a common understanding*: Team-based problem solving is extremely effective but requires a common understanding of the issue. Cause-effect diagrams are a very practical collaboration technique.

- *Identify how problems affect the business*: Knowledge of this enables people to focus on the most important problems first and make informed decisions.

- *Find root causes*: This helps maximize the effect of your changes.

- *Eliminate vicious cycles* (negative reinforcing loops): Break vicious cycles or turn them into positive reinforcing loops (good stuff leading to more good stuff, instead of bad stuff leading to more bad stuff).

Cause-effect diagrams are useful, but the key point is really the problem solving approach itself: the questions asked and the resulting conversations and insights. You might not even need to draw the actual diagram, just picturing it in your head as you talk can be enough.

This structured problem-solving approach is useful in just about any context —such as coaching a friend or improving your own life. Or even improving the world!

CHAPTER 21

Final Words

OK, it has been a long journey. Now let's wrap it up!

In Part I you learned about our project—how we work and what we've learned along the way. In Part II you learned more about the specific techniques used in the project. Now what?

If you're interested in more material of this sort, then feel free to keep an eye on my blog, at http://blog.crisp.se/author/henrikkniberg. You also can give feedback or participate in discussions about this book on http://pragprog.com/book/hklean/lean-from-the-trenches.

It's tempting to give you a long list of further reading. But I won't do that. You've read enough for the moment; it's time to put this book down and get back into your own trenches!

Knowledge doesn't stick unless you practice. So, think about what you learned from this book and how this knowledge might come to use in your context. Then go experiment!

Glossary: How We Avoid Buzzword Bingo

Much of the Lean and Agile lingo sounds strange to normal people, especially non-English speakers. (Everyone on the PUST project speaks Swedish.) Words like *product backlog*, *retrospective*, *user story*, *velocity*, *Scrum master*, and *story points* can seriously alienate nontechies.

So, I've tried to de-buzzwordify as much as possible in this project. There's no need to alienate people unnecessarily. Being careful about our choice of terminology has turned out to be very helpful, so let me share our glossary with you.

Needless to say, this chapter is most relevant to the Swedish readers.

Our Term	Literal Translation to English	What We Meant (Corresponding Buzzwords/Synonyms)
Processförbättringsmöte	Process improvement meeting	Sprint retrospective
Leverabel	Deliverable	Feature, product backlog item
Kundleverabel	Customer deliverable	User story (as opposed to tech stories and other noncustomer stuff)
Funktionsområde	Feature area	Epic, theme
Teamledare	Team lead	Scrum master
Projekttavla	Project board	Project-level Kanban board
Teamtavla	Team board	Team-level Kanban/Scrum hybrid board

The term *leverabel* was especially useful. Previously, the term *krav* (= *requirements*) was used to mean just about anything. Now there is a clear distinction between *leverabel* and *funktionsområde*.

Index

Be Agile

Don't just "do" agile; you want to *be* agile. We'll show you how.

The best agile book isn't a book: *Agile in a Flash* is a unique deck of index cards that fit neatly in your pocket. You can tape them to the wall. Spread them out on your project table. Get stains on them over lunch. These cards are meant to be used, not just read.

Jeff Langr and Tim Ottinger
(110 pages) ISBN: 9781934356715. $15
http://pragprog.com/titles/olag

Here are three simple truths about software development:

1. You can't gather all the requirements up front. 2. The requirements you do gather will change. 3. There is always more to do than time and money will allow.

Those are the facts of life. But you can deal with those facts (and more) by becoming a fierce software-delivery professional, capable of dispatching the most dire of software projects and the toughest delivery schedules with ease and grace.

Jonathan Rasmusson
(280 pages) ISBN: 9781934356586. $34.95
http://pragprog.com/titles/jtrap

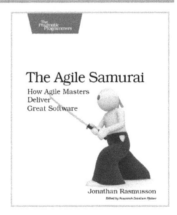

Get Results

Reading about new techniques is one thing, making them work in your company and on your team is another matter entirely. Here's the help you need.

If you work with people, you need this book. Learn to read co-workers' and users' *patterns of resistance* and dismantle their objections. With these techniques and strategies you can master the art of evangelizing and help your organization adopt your solutions.

Terrence Ryan
(200 pages) ISBN: 9781934356609. $32.95
http://pragprog.com/titles/trevan

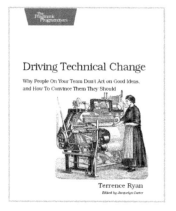

Discover how to coach your team to become more Agile. *Agile Coaching* de-mystifies agile practices—it's a practical guide to creating strong agile teams. Packed with useful tips from practicing agile coaches Rachel Davies and Liz Sedley, this book gives you coaching tools that you can apply whether you are a project manager, a technical lead, or working in a software team.

Rachel Davies and Liz Sedley
(248 pages) ISBN: 9781934356432. $34.95
http://pragprog.com/titles/sdcoach

More on Agile Development

Working on embedded systems or on your own? This is how it's done, the agile way.

Still chasing bugs and watching your code deteriorate?
Think TDD is only for desktop or web apps? It's not:
TDD is for you, the embedded C programmer. TDD
helps you prevent defects and build software with a
long useful life. This is the first book to teach the hows
and whys of TDD for C programmers.

James W. Grenning
(384 pages) ISBN: 9781934356623. $34.95
http://pragprog.com/titles/jgade

Want to be a better developer? This book collects the
personal habits, ideas, and approaches of successful
agile software developers and presents them in a series
of short, easy-to-digest tips.

You'll learn how to improve your software development
process, see what real agile practices feel like, avoid
the common temptations that kill projects, and keep
agile practices in balance.

Venkat Subramaniam and Andy Hunt
(208 pages) ISBN: 9780974514086. $29.95
http://pragprog.com/titles/pad

Think Better

Want to concentrate more effectively, and learn how to take advantage of your brain's wiring? We've got you covered.

Do you ever look at the clock and wonder where the day went? You spent all this time at work and didn't come close to getting everything done. Tomorrow, try something new. Use the Pomodoro Technique, originally developed by Francesco Cirillo, to work in focused sprints throughout the day. In *Pomodoro Technique Illustrated*, Staffan Nöteberg shows you how to organize your work to accomplish more in less time. There's no need for expensive software or fancy planners. You can get started with nothing more than a piece of paper, a pencil, and a kitchen timer.

Staffan Nöteberg
(144 pages) ISBN: 9781934356500. $24.95
http://pragprog.com/titles/snfocus

Software development happens in your head. Not in an editor, IDE, or design tool. You're well educated on how to work with software and hardware, but what about *wetware*—our own brains? Learning new skills and new technology is critical to your career, and it's all in your head.

In this book by Andy Hunt, you'll learn how our brains are wired, and how to take advantage of your brain's architecture. You'll learn new tricks and tips to learn more, faster, and retain more of what you learn.

You need a pragmatic approach to thinking and learning. You need to *Refactor Your Wetware.*

Andy Hunt
(288 pages) ISBN: 9781934356050. $34.95
http://pragprog.com/titles/ahptl

The Pragmatic Bookshelf

The Pragmatic Bookshelf features books written by developers for developers. The titles continue the well-known Pragmatic Programmer style and continue to garner awards and rave reviews. As development gets more and more difficult, the Pragmatic Programmers will be there with more titles and products to help you stay on top of your game.

Visit Us Online

This Book's Home Page
http://pragprog.com/titles/hklean
Source code from this book, errata, and other resources. Come give us feedback, too!

Register for Updates
http://pragprog.com/updates
Be notified when updates and new books become available.

Join the Community
http://pragprog.com/community
Read our weblogs, join our online discussions, participate in our mailing list, interact with our wiki, and benefit from the experience of other Pragmatic Programmers.

New and Noteworthy
http://pragprog.com/news
Check out the latest pragmatic developments, new titles and other offerings.

Save on the eBook

Save on the eBook versions of this title. Owning the paper version of this book entitles you to purchase the electronic versions at a terrific discount.

PDFs are great for carrying around on your laptop—they are hyperlinked, have color, and are fully searchable. Most titles are also available for the iPhone and iPod touch, Amazon Kindle, and other popular e-book readers.

Buy now at *http://pragprog.com/coupon*

Contact Us

Online Orders:	*http://pragprog.com/catalog*
Customer Service:	*support@pragprog.com*
International Rights:	*translations@pragprog.com*
Academic Use:	*academic@pragprog.com*
Write for Us:	*http://pragprog.com/write-for-us*
Or Call:	+1 800-699-7764

Lightning Source UK Ltd.
Milton Keynes UK
UKHW032057130319
338863UK00014B/39/P

9 781934 356852